I0579283

DEDICATION

To Tie, who has been a friend and a sister, especially when I needed one most.

What is the Wyrdwood Project? Learn more.
(http://wyrdwoodangel.com/about/)

Hexing the Moon

by Angel Leigh McCoy

PRELUDE

Bella Rosenblum glared out the window at the apartment building's swimming pool two stories below, where a gaggle of children splashed and shrieked with laughter. Their piercing screeches tweaked Bella's nerves. She drew the curtains closed, shutting out both the sunlight and most of the noise.

Truth was, her nerves had seen better days. Ever since the Fomor curse had been broken, she had barely slept. She spent her days hunched over a scrying bowl, gathering nuggets of information as if her life depended on it. She wasn't convinced it didn't. Returning to the coffee table, she lowered herself to the floor, despite the complaint from her knees, and sat cross-legged. Working her magick indoors never turned out as well as when she was out in nature, but beggars couldn't be choosers. The moment she'd heard how Rioghain had used Viviane and Colin to get a Fomor into Apfallon, she knew she'd sealed her fate. The Apfallonians blamed Viviane for their predicament. Imagine how they must feel about the woman who had created the circumstances under which Colin and Viviane fell in love.

They had all just been pawns in Rioghain's plot to

plunder Bella's homeland.

Morbid curiosity drove Bella back to the scrying bowl. She dumped the old water into a bucket and poured fresh from the crystal pitcher. She sprinkled sea salt and lavender on the surface and swirled it with her finger to push the buds to the outer edges. As the magick poured from her, streaming into the water, she focused her mind and whispered, "Lenore Gliton."

It took longer than usual for the water to clear. Scrying into Apfallon was never easy and often impossible. Bella could never see inside Gliton Manor, but she got lucky. Lenore had left the manor and was standing at the railing of a sailing ship.

High above the ground, the ship flew, pushed along by a breeze. Held aloft by three hot air balloons, the galleon made no sound until a sudden and thunderous whoosh signaled a blaze of fire meant to heat the air in the central balloon.

The landscape of Apfallon lay a hundred feet below—so precious to Bella that the sight of it brought tears to her eyes. Green hills rolled to the horizon, decorated with forests, rivers, lakes, and the signs of Apfallonian life: roads, farms, churches, mills, and homes. The people of Apfallon paused in their tasks to gaze up into the sky at the passing ship, point, wave, and call out happy greetings. A shepherd did a lively jig for the pleasure of the ship's passenger, Lenore—Bella's mother.

Lenore didn't react to her citizens because her attention was on the horizon. She squinted and raised a hand to shield her eyes from the sunlight, though she needn't have. The black pool amassing on the southern shore of Apfallon stood out like an oozing, gangrenous wound.

The anchor descended to the ground. The sound of its thick chains carried a metallic violence that made Bella shiver. The ship eased its forward momentum and came to a halt with a jolt.

After a few moments, the pilot came to stand beside Lenore. Bella knew her name was Aditi. Of Anggitay heritage, she was humanoid from the waist up and horse from there down. She was voluptuous, her curves full and feminine. Her skin had seen much sunshine over the years and appeared to have fallen in love with its warmth. She had a scruffy head of light brown hair with bangs that hung low enough to cover her eyes if she let them. Most importantly, they covered the stunted horn in the center of her forehead.

Others of her race grew a single swirled horn, like unicorns. Aditi's had come in crooked and stopped growing when it was little more than a nub. When Bella had first met the young Anggitay, she'd been hiding in a cellar, crying because the other children had cruelly teased her.

Aditi had overcome her lack of traditional beauty by being the best at everything she undertook. She excelled in school and became the youngest pilot in the Apfallonian airship brigade. She wore the colors of Gliton, azure and white—a tailored long-coat that lay in pleats upon her back and a white blouse left open to her navel. The curves of her heavy breasts kept the blouse taut.

"Can I get you anything, Lady?" Aditi asked, her voice throaty, her tone businesslike.

Lenore didn't take her eyes off the horizon. "We can't get any closer?"

"Not safely," the pilot replied. "I prefer not to tempt the Fates."

"May I use your spyglass?"

"Of course."

Bella already knew what Lenore would see, but she sucked in a sharp breath when the images came into the water. The black pool was an army. The Fomor had arrived in Apfallon armed and itching for a fight. Wearing black and gray armor, they swarmed. Many got down on their hands and knees and kissed the ground. The Fomor came in a variety of body types, some as monstrous as bugganes, some as elegant as the Thu. They had not advanced beyond the shore, but Bella knew it was only a matter of time. Her blood ran cold, and reflexively, she broke the surface tension on the water, ending the scrying. With growing dread, she put her head in her hands and wished she knew how to stop the war.

CHAPTER 1

"I believe in everything until it's disproved.
So I believe in fairies, the myths, dragons.
It all exists even if it's in your mind.
Who's to say that dreams and nightmares
aren't as real as the here and now?"
—John Lennon—

I stood at the threshold to purgatory—Gehenna. A long hallway stretched out before me—the proverbial tunnel. The light at the end of it did little to illuminate my way. Instead, it whitewashed the details of what lay ahead. The back of my neck twitched, and my shoulders clenched in dread. I felt certain someone—or some thing—was watching me.

Oddly—or perhaps not—the corridor reminded me of Vince Malum Residential Living Center. It made sense that my Purgatory would resemble my own personal Hell. Doors lined the walls, and everything sat askew, as if tilted or twisted. I had no desire whatsoever to explore what lay beyond those doors. I tightened my grip on the fireplace poker in my hand and kept my focus on the path ahead.

Something brushed the back of my shoulder, and I jumped. I nearly turned to face it, but I knew the rules. Colin had explained them very clearly—ad nauseum. I must not look back until I was in the light.

"No matter what," he'd said.

"What will happen if I do?" I'd asked.

"You'll lose your way." That was all he would say about it, but his dire tone made the warning clear.

"Where will you be?"

Colin had said, "I'll be waiting for you in the light."

It wasn't much more comforting in retrospect. Though my mind was telling me to move forward toward the light, my legs weren't on board. They refused to move.

Something hissed behind me. My breath hitched.

Eyes wide, I strained to hear.

Whispers. All around me.

"It's her."

"Sweetness."

"She's here."

And those were just the tidbits I could make out. A hum of voices all around me wove together to create a blanket that threatened to suffocate me.

Of their own accord, my feet started moving. Panic had me by the neck. I broke into a run, making a break for the light—the mysterious light that held unknown danger—and maybe my Colin.

A sharp pain erupted in my ankle, then another on the back of my head. Something had hold of my hair. I wrapped my hand around the snagged lock even as I leaned back. My feet kept going, and I almost went down. I yanked myself free just as I reached my tipping point and somehow managed to both stay upright and remain facing forward.

I swung the iron poker wildly behind me, not knowing at what. The poker didn't contact anything, and I felt the strain in my wrist as it whipped around at an awkward angle.

The whispers snuck in around me. "Pretty."

"Golden."

"She's ours."

I shouted, "Get away from me!" My center dropped an inch or two, and I readied to run again. I gritted my teeth and locked my gaze on the light at the end of the hallway—the tunnel. It didn't seem any closer than it had been when I'd first arrived, but at least I wasn't turned around.

A sibilant wind blew up from behind me, lifting the hem of my coat and the ends of my hair. It was hot and smelled like the sewer. So thick, it made me gag. I put my free hand over my nose and mouth.

Something tugged at my coat sleeve.

That was it. I was done. I pulled free and ran full bore toward the light. If there was anything beyond it—inside it—it had better be ready to catch me because I wasn't stopping.

I sprinted. The sound of my feet slamming on the tile echoed in the empty hall. The rasp of my breath gained speed as the hallway stretched and what physical endurance I had was put to the test.

The beings with their grabby hands and terrifying whispers kept pace with me. I slapped at fingers that grabbed at me, felt claws cut into my legs, arms, and scalp. They herded me like a cow toward slaughter. The poor cow thought salvation lay at the end of the corridor. Going back was never an option.

I barreled forward for what seemed like an eternity, ignoring the pain in my side, the burn in my throat, and the fear that I didn't have it in me to continue.

My steps slowed to stumbling, and I leaned forward to keep whatever momentum I had going.

"Colin!" I cried, wanting—needing—help.

I had to stop. Black dots danced at the edge of my vision. I put my hands on my knees and panted hot, fetid air. I couldn't get enough. I was suffocating. My legs gave out, and my vision went white.

The last things I remembered were the dirty tile floor rising up toward me, a sickening vertigo, and a single thought:

Being dead sucks.

❀❀❀

CHAPTER 2

Thirteen days earlier...

He saw me before I saw him. Unfortunately.

"Vivi!" he called. "Viviane!"

I'd know his voice anywhere. *Richard.* He was getting out of a cab in front of the haven. I had just come out of the forest, higher on the ridge, on the path near Cedar House.

My grandfather had warned me that Dr. Richard Reuter had been trying to contact me, despite—or maybe because of—the fact that he'd lost his license to practice medicine for his abuse of our doctor-patient relationship. I clicked my teeth together, and a nervous vibration started up at the back of my neck.

In the time since I'd left the Vince Malum Residential Living Center—a fancy, misleading name for a mental institution—I hadn't had time to process how I felt about Richard. I'd been too busy, and if I were honest, too eager to avoid looking back.

Richard was a symbol of my unhappy past. He'd been my psychiatrist for so long—a fixture in my day-to-day life since I was a teen. He knew me better than anyone else in the world—even better than my fiancé Colin did. That made him dangerous, especially since he'd proven he didn't have my best interests at heart.

"Hey!" Richard called again, waving to me. "Vivi!" His casual attire underscored the fact that he was no longer a licensed professional. I wasn't used to seeing him in jeans and an untucked polo shirt of sky blue. It was, I knew, his favorite color, and it made him seem deceptively approachable.

I had hoped I'd never see Richard again, but that wasn't very adult of me. Or realistic. Having to face Richard was well-earned karma. I began a slow descent toward the Lost Lambs parking lot but couldn't bring myself to return Richard's smile.

The taxi driver pulled a small suitcase from the trunk, and Richard picked it up.

Jake Lamb appeared, descending the stairs from Holly House. I couldn't see his face, but his shoulders held tension. He reached Richard before I did, and I saw him tell the taxi driver to wait. *Uh oh,* I thought.

Richard and Jake stood facing one another. Richard offered to shake hands, but Jake ignored it. *Double uh oh,* I thought. Jake wasn't even trying to be polite.

By the time I got close enough to hear it, Richard was saying, "...no right. I just want to speak to Vivi...Viviane."

Jake's voice was low, barely audible to me, and as serious as I'd ever heard him be. He said, "You're not her doctor anymore."

"Maybe not," said Richard, then he looked up at me and raised the volume to be sure I heard him, "but we've been friends for many years. I just need to know she's okay. I heard about Gisèle, Vivi. I am so sorry." That wasn't his p-doc voice. It was his pleading, promise-me-we-still-have-a-connection voice.

I kept my pace slow and steady, descending the hillside toward them without comment. My mind was running circles around itself as question after question rose to join the race. *What did he want from me? Why was he there? What was I going to say to him? Could I forgive him? Did I even want to?*

Richard made a move to walk toward me, to meet me halfway, but Jake put out a hand to stop him. They exchanged a look, and Jake shook his head.

"You need to go," Jake said. "If Viviane wants to see you, we can arrange it, but ambushing her like this is unacceptable."

"I only want five minutes." Richard looked up at me again. "Just five minutes, Vivi. That's all. Then I'll go. I promise." He took another step toward me.

I looked from him to Jake and back again. Jake's opinion on the matter was obvious. He'd throw Richard in the taxi's trunk and send it back to Peoria.

A little voice inside me said, *He helped you. For many years, he helped you.*

A second one argued, *He used you. He collected your life like a series of short stories he planned to publish as an anthology. Amusement for the masses, by Dr. Richard Reuter.*

The first countered, *He was your first love.*

The second huffed, *He knew the body they found wasn't Colin, and he lied about it.*

I stopped fifteen feet away, arms crossed on my chest, and asked, "What do you want, Richard?"

His mouth worked like a fish out of water. "I...I...I just wanted to talk to you. How are you? You look good. Your hair's getting long."

"I'm better," I told him, and it was one of the truest things I'd ever said.

"Good," he replied. "I'm really glad." He smiled, and I resented it. He continued, "I wanted to come to your mom's funeral, but...something came up." He glanced sideways at Jake, a look I read to indicate that what had come up was Jake telling him to stay away. I hadn't known Jake had done so, but it didn't surprise me.

It was my turn to ask how he was, but I wasn't sure I gave a damn. If it hadn't been for my family's lawyer, I'd still be stuck at Malum having daily sessions with him and thinking I was crazy.

"I'm not crazy," I told him.

He nodded. "I never said you were."

I said, "You didn't have to say it. You...believed it. Enabled it. Encouraged and exaggerated it."

"Vivi, I—"

I cut him off. "You should go."

"Please, Vivi. I—"

Then, Jake cut him off. "You heard the lady. Time to go." Jake opened the back door to the taxi. "Don't make me call the police."

Richard looked like a trapped animal, eyes bouncing from Jake to the taxi to me to his own hands—those hands that I'd held so many times, that had rubbed my back while I cried over my dramas, that had set the metronome to ticking. Even from where I was, I could see those hands were shaking.

"Vivi," Richard said, "I love you." He didn't look at me as he said it, and he moved toward the cab. He tossed his bag into the backseat, then faced me again. "Did you get the letters I sent to your old address?"

I didn't answer. Abram had mentioned letters, but I hadn't seen them.

Richard continued, "Let's have dinner some evening—my treat. Call or text me. My number hasn't changed. If you ever need to talk, I'm here for you."

"Time to go," Jake said, and his tone brooked no argument.

Defeated, Richard got into the taxi. Jake closed the door and banged twice on the roof. The taxi slowly backed out and drove away.

Only when it was out of sight did I look at Jake and realize he was watching me. He said, "I think you should get a restraining order."

I nodded once, turned around, and headed back up the path. He was probably right.

❀❀❀

CHAPTER 3

That day, everything changed. After Richard left, I returned to my room in Cedar House and began the long job of processing what he'd done to me and how I felt about it. I found answers to some of the questions banging around in my head and started to comprehend exactly how badly he'd betrayed my confidence. He had allowed me to believe my fiancé was dead—though he knew damn well the body they'd found wasn't Colin. He'd written a book about my life and my treatments, including the most personal moments, and it came out later that he'd already begun shopping it around to publishers. The fact that he'd given me a fake name was beside the point.

To make matters worse, he'd conspired to keep me medicated and off-kilter so he could control me—theoretically to gather more material for his book—even going so far as to ask me to move in with him. The whole idea disgusted me.

I'd trusted him.

The biggest conclusion I came to as I stood by my window gazing out at the ocean on the horizon was that Richard would never go away until I myself stood up to him. As an intermediary, Jake was effective, but only temporarily. I had to deal with Richard myself, face-to-face and with my head and heart as clear as I could get them. Which meant I wasn't ready.

He'd conditioned me well over years of therapy. A part of me still felt I needed him. Like a child's security blanket, he was the one I'd always run to when the world was falling apart. He'd been my confidante, my crutch, and my mentor for so long that even after everything, I found it hard not to think of calling him in my darkest hours.

No. I didn't need Richard any more. If nothing else, my life had expanded so far beyond him that I couldn't tell him half of what was happening to me. He didn't know about or believe in magick. He couldn't see the magickal races through his normal human eyes, and he'd never think I was anything other than delusional.

Working through all that exhausted me, and I lay down for a nap. It wasn't long before I passed out, and when I awoke, it was in a groggy haze. The first thing I saw was what I interpreted to be orange curtains moving in a breeze.

An eye. A bulbous, round eye with a black center. Staring at me.

I blinked, frowned, and blinked again. My mind caught up.

"Holy shit!" I pushed away from it and slid right off the edge of the bed, landing on my ass, banging my head on the bedside dresser, and pulling the blankets down on top of me.

A deep roll of laughter applauded my reaction. *Simon.*

My vision cleared. Floating in the air over the bed was a goldfish. A large goldfish—the size of a big dog. I'd confused its long, fanned fins as curtains. They rippled in non-existent water, keeping the creature afloat.

"Your Sight has improved since last I saw ye," said a familiar voice that came from the fish.

"Simon?"

"Yes! Clever girl. 'Tis I. Glad to see you're still alive."

"You're a fucking goldfish?" I blurted.

Simon laughed again, the sound rippling along his fins. "Don't judge. This is my pretty form. I have others that'd make you shit your drawers."

I untangled myself from the bedding. I'd known Simon since I was thirteen, and not once had I ever seen him. He'd been my invisible, imaginary friend—until recently when I'd learned that others could hear him too. And there he was in all his strange and magickal glory.

It hit me fully that it was him and that I was happy he was back. Then, a wave of anger overshadowed my joy.

"Where have you been?" I asked. "You missed so much. I needed you. Mom...is dead."

"I know, lass. I'm so sorry about that. I was on a mission. Important thing is I'm here now."

I got to my knees, then to my feet.

Simon swam backward a bit to give me room. "I have something to tell you."

A knock sounded on my door.

I looked at the door, then at Simon. He was already beginning to fade out of sight, like the Cheshire Cat. His eyes were the last to disappear.

"Never mind," he said. "Looks like you're about to find out the hard way."

Mixed feelings jumbled into a knot in my belly. I was in a raft on rapids without an oar.

"Come in!" I called, and the door opened to reveal Booker, a young Native American man in the final year of his teens. He stuck his head in and said, "Y'got a visitor, V. Jake sent me up to get you. They're in the Holly house."

"Who is it?"

"Some old lady. I dunno."

"Is it Lenore?"

Booker shook his head. "I dunno." He slipped out of sight and was gone.

I didn't know many old ladies except those at Malum. I decided it was probably Lenore, my great-grandmother and one of the leaders in Apfallon—a magickal pocket realm where all kinds of supernatural beings lived. I smoothed my clothes and checked my hair in the mirror.

"You coming?" I asked Simon.

He replied, a voice out of nowhere, "I'm right behind you. Don't keep her waiting."

I scooted down to the living room in Holly House.

Ayu, the haven's domestic manager, was stoking a fire in the fireplace, and Jake was seated in a chair facing me. An older woman sat on the couch, her back to me.

It wasn't Lenore.

Jake saw me, said something, and nodded in my direction.

Bella Rosenblum turned to face me. My mouth fell open. She and Jake both stood.

"Hello, Viviane," Bella said, holding out both her hands for mine. "How delightful to see you." Her hair had more silver in it, overcoming what was left of its auburn blush, and her face had more wrinkles. The sparkle had not left her eyes, however.

She wore a lavender button-up sweater over tailored black pants. As I looked at her, the Sight slowly revealed her true self to me. Her features became more fae, her ears more delicate. The breeze that always seemed to accompany her ruffled her curls.

I walked to her and took her hands. "Hi." I hadn't seen Bella since the battle with Nathan at her house in Illinois. I hadn't seen her since I'd learned that she was my grandmother. Her presence took me back into the past—my third trip that day.

She looked me up and down. "You're doing well?"

Jake mumbled something about letting us talk in

private and left.

I said, "My mother…is gone."

"I heard what happened," she replied, her voice heavy with sorrow. She pulled me to the couch by my hands and sat without letting go. "That must have been so difficult for you. We have a lot to talk about. I owe you an explanation."

I sat with her and said. "I know that you're…my grandmother."

Bella took a deep breath and let it out with a huff. "Good," she said. "I wasn't sure how I was going to break that to you. I'm sorry I couldn't tell you sooner. It was for your own good."

"You hid to protect Mom, right?"

"That's right." Bella squeezed my hands. Hers were surprisingly strong. "It's a long story. How much do you know?"

I replied, "Only that my father was a Fomor and that Mom fell in love with him. You were afraid he'd take me from her, right?"

"Your father knew that you could break the Fomor curse. You're the first child to have both Tuatha dé Danaan and Fomorian blood in many generations." She pronounced the names of the races with a Celtic lilt that rooted them in ancient history.

I leaned forward, "I *did* break it."

"I know. It's okay." Bella's expression was sympathetic. "Don't worry. You'll get a chance to fix it."

"I will?"

"That's why I'm here. To help you."

"Everyone thinks you're dead. Abram, Lenore..."

Bella's mouth tightened into a grim line. "I know. Thank you for keeping my secret. Now that I'm back, I'll explain it all to Lenore, but your grandfather can never know the truth. He wouldn't understand, and it would only hurt him."

She was right. Learning that his wife, his one true love, had not died, but had actually been in hiding just miles away—for a decade or more—would crush Abram.

"I'm sorry," she said, "about my role in the accident."

It took me a second to understand what she was talking about, then my memories of the car wreck returned.

"It was you," I said, breathless. "On the lake shore. You were the woman."

Bella nodded. "You were never in any real danger," she said. "Well, not much."

"The man who jumped out in front of us... He was with you?"

"It was orchestrated so we could get Colin into hiding. He'd begun to break out of the amnesia. His step-brother had come sniffing around, and we had to move quickly. It was crude, I know. I'm sorry you were involved, but it had to happen away from the Center. We had no other alternative."

I studied her, my jaw tense. "I thought he was dead. That was the worst time of my life. Why couldn't you just tell me?"

"Sweetie, your Sight had only just begun to manifest. I couldn't risk it. If you'd reacted poorly, you might have gone to the police, or worse, doubted your own sanity."

"Well," I said with more than a little snark, "that happened anyway."

She licked her lips and stared down at her hands. "It was a mess." Quietly, she said again, "I'm sorry."

I wasn't ready to let her off the hook, but it all felt like water under the bridge—like a different lifetime. I asked, "Why did you help Colin, anyway?"

"Mmm, good question." Bella stared into the fire a moment before continuing. "The only reason was to safeguard you and Apfallon. When he first showed up, I thought he was looking for you, and I almost killed him on the spot. When he told me he wanted nothing to do with his parents' agenda, not with the grudge against the Thu nor the politics of Gehenna, I didn't believe him."

"You thought he was lying?"

"Yes, until I suggested amnesia as a way to mask himself permanently. I said it to test him, told him he could start a new life—a Reality-based life. I promised his family would never find him. If he hadn't accepted, I'd have killed him. But he did accept. Leapt at it even. That convinced me he was telling the truth."

I was seeing Bella in a whole new light. I knew most of the story from Colin, but I'd never imagined it from her point of view. Suddenly all those times she'd tried to warn me away from Colin made sense.

I laughed.

"What's so funny?" she asked.

"You must have been chewing your nails when Colin and I started spending time together."

"Oh," she said, eyes widening. "Believe me. I was. I nearly moved him to a different facility, except I needed to stay close to Gisèle. Once I realized the power he had over you, I was locked into helping him stay hidden. For your sake. You two... Your love was a force of nature."

We laughed together, my grandmother and I. It was unexpectedly satisfying.

Bella—whose real name was Moira—and I talked for an hour about all that had happened in the past, about my Fomor father, my Thu roots, and my time at Malum.

Eventually, Bella said, "I want to show you something." She released my hands and reached for a tote bag resting on the floor beside her. She pulled it into her lap and opened it. From inside, she withdrew a bowl, a thermos, one plastic bag of what looked like rock salt, and another with lavender buds. She set each item on the coffee table in front of her.

"What's all this?" I asked.

She opened the thermos and poured water from it into the bowl. "Our family has the gift of remote viewing."

"I've done that!" I announced.

Bella frowned and studied me for a moment, then chuckled, her face relaxing. "I shouldn't be surprised. You're strong. A late bloomer, but all the more powerful for it." She patted my thigh.

I said, "Does using objects like this help?"

"In certain situations, yes." Bella sprinkled salt upon the water. "This spell is called 'Scrying,' and it helps me see people who would otherwise be obscured—those protected by magick or whom I've never met." She took a pinch of lavender buds and dropped them into the bowl. "You could say it boosts the signal, I suppose." With a sly look, she set everything aside, then swirled her finger in the water, mixing it. "I need you to be quiet while I do this. Gaze into the bowl with your Sight, and you will see what I see."

I sat up and squared my hips and shoulders. "What are we going to see?" I asked.

"Wait for it...," she murmured, then, "Shhh..."

I felt it when Bella's energy shifted, when the magick began to hum. It called to something inside me and set my spine to tingling. My breathing slowed and synchronized with hers.

Bella whispered a few quiet words—foreign words I didn't recognize—then finished with two I did. "Lenore Gliton."

Her gaze was locked on the bowl, her expression slack, unblinking. Movement appeared on the surface of the water, and an image coalesced.

Lenore stood at a wooden railing high above the ground, dwarfed by the unbelievable creature standing beside her—half woman and half horse, a centaur from my mythology books. The centaur was terrifying and yet civilized, dressed in an old-fashioned military-style coat, left unbuttoned. A white fitted blouse was the only other clothing she wore, her breasts heavy inside it, dark nipples visible through the thin fabric.

The centaur said, "I expected more."

"Yes," replied Lenore, eyes on the horizon. "But it could just be the first wave. We need to get our defenses in place."

"They didn't waste any time."

"They've been planning this for decades. Maybe longer."

In the distance, a black stain spread across the horizon. As I studied it, I saw that it was actually a teeming mass of people—of beings who wrapped themselves in shadows. The Fomor army had arrived at Apfallon's border.

"They'll establish their base camp there," said Lenore, expression hard. "Maybe send out scouts. Maybe not."

The centaur said, "We have to stop them before they get to the forest."

"Yes." Lenore's tone was heavy.

Beside me, Bella said, "Or they will destroy everything in their path."

"Can they take Apfallon?" asked the centaur.

Lenore sighed. "Not without a fight," she said. "Not without a fight."

Bella and I watched a moment longer. Lenore and the centaur were buffeted by a gust of wind, their hair flying about their heads. Upon the centaur's forehead, I saw something I didn't understand—a deformity just in the center. It looked like a bone spur, growing out at an angle. Then her bangs fell back over it.

"Take me home," said Lenore.

The centaur turned away, her hooves clomping loudly on wood.

Bella put her finger into the water and stirred. The magick dissipated, and the image disappeared.

"This is all my fault," I said.

"No," said Bella. "It's not your fault. This situation has been brewing for a long time. It was foretold. What matters is how we handle it now that it's here."

I rubbed my face and pushed my hair back. "It's so medieval. So primitive."

Bella considered that then replied, "The Fomor hold a grudge. From their point of view, they've been kept from their homeland for millennia."

"But no one alive today was responsible for that."

"Not directly, I suppose, but we are our own ancestors."

"Reincarnation," I said. "But I'm not responsible for what I did in another life."

"Aren't you?"

I shifted uneasily on the couch. "Maybe it's time to extend the olive branch? Reach out? Make amends."

Bella chewed on her lip.

I continued, "They need to talk to each other. I mean, I've met the leaders of both, and they're intelligent, rational people."

Bella commented, "Intelligent, rational people amassing an army with every intention of killing anything that gets in their way."

"That's a lose-lose situation. If only someone could get them to see that."

"No matter what," Bella said, "we have to protect Apfallon. It cannot fall to the Fomor. Even if we have to kill them all."

My stomach churned as I desperately tried to think. I asked, "Can you show me Gehenna? Show me Rio? If we can see what they're doing, we can get out ahead of them."

Bella folded her hands in her lap. "I can't. Gehenna is not a physical realm. It's a spirit realm. My scrying will not penetrate it."

I said, "I've been in Rio's head before. Maybe I...,"

but Bella shook her head.

"Not from here," she said. "If you were *in* Gehenna, you might be able to reach her. That realm vibrates on a different level."

I stood and began to pace. "You said I'd get a chance to fix it. How?"

Bella nodded, her silver curls dancing with the movement and the invisible breeze that never left her. "I don't know," she said. "I don't know." Sorrow weighted her words. "But you have to."

CHAPTER 4

The doorbell tolled, interrupting my freak-out. Bella and I both looked at the door.

"Who now?" I asked without expecting an answer. The thought that it might be Richard made my spine tense.

The bell rang again, and Ayu hustled out of the back hall. I immediately felt guilty for hesitating.

"I can get it," I offered.

Ayu waved me off. "I've got it, Viviane." She went straight to the door and opened it.

Late afternoon sunlight streamed in, silhouetting a short, slim figure. The back-lighting revealed her body outline through the white peasant skirt and blouse she wore. It shone in her pale hair, making her seem thoroughly ethereal. I knew immediately who it was.

Ayu greeted Amalia with reverence, almost bowing as she gestured the Midwife inside.

Amalia entered with a purposeful stride and came straight toward me. Her very presence intimidated me, but then I saw what she carried. In her arms was a small bundle—a wiggling, fresh-faced bundle of baby. Ivy had one fist in the air and a handful of Amalia's hair in the other.

A wave of emotion flowed through me at the sight of Agate's baby, the tiny Ivy that I'd helped bring into the world. So happy was I to see her that I nearly forgot it was creepy Amalia who was holding her.

"It's Ivy," I said.

Amalia walked right up to me and offered me the baby. "Take her. She's hungry."

I transferred her into my arms and held her tiny body close. Wrapped loosely in a white silk cloth, she squirmed against me, fussing.

"Sit down," Amalia commanded, putting pressure on my shoulder.

I obeyed.

Bella moved out of the way.

"This is Ivy," I told Bella. "Her mother died in childbirth. Jake and I were there when she was in labor. There was—" I felt Amalia's hand unbutton the top button on my blouse. I leaned away from her. "Excuse me!"

Undaunted, she continued. "The child is hungry," she said, as if that explained everything. She had three buttons undone already.

"Wait a minute. Hold on." I tried to push her hands away without dropping Ivy. I swatted at her fingers. "I can't feed her."

Ivy began to cry, short mewling bursts.

With a roll of her sky-blue eyes, Amalia pressed her palm to my forehead. I felt a spark there, like static electricity. It traveled down my neck and into my chest.

"You are part human," she said. "You will nourish her."

My body changed, became puffy all over in a moment, as if filled with energy.

Amalia took a step back and crossed her arms, staring a challenge down at me.

Ivy's cry had grown more intense, her face pinched, her eyes wet. She nuzzled my breast through my bra, my nipple. The sensation made me woozy. I stared down at the baby.

A stain was spreading on my bra, and I was on the verge of panic.

Bella saved the day. She rested a warm hand on my shoulder and said with much more kindness than Amalia had shown, "It's okay. You're okay. It's magick. You can do this." She smiled down at me. "Amalia wouldn't ask if it weren't right for the baby. Go on."

Ivy was wailing and bright red in the face. I could have handed her back to Amalia. I could have refused, but I didn't want to. In that moment, I wanted nothing more than to nurse Ivy. I pushed aside my bra. My nipple was swollen and wet with milk. I positioned Ivy, and she latched on like a pro. The wails stopped, and she rested her hand with its tiny fingers, tiny nails, against my breast.

I don't know how long we stayed like that, no one speaking. I was overcome with feelings I didn't have words for—with love for Ivy. My conscious mind struggled against the primal urges that swelled up in me. It was a high like none I'd ever experienced.

Once Ivy had had her fill, she dozed in my arms. I pulled my bra and shirt back over myself, turned her upright against my shoulder, and rocked her. It was the most natural thing, holding her against me.

Amalia sat down beside me, her attention on Bella's scrying bowl. She leaned forward and blew across the water. It rippled, then cleared, and an image appeared in it. Bella drew nearer to see.

I gasped. "Is that?"

Bella said, "Gisèle."

My late mother, Gisèle, was seated on the edge of a white-draped canopy bed in a pool of light. Shadows filled the edges of the room. Her hands were folded together and tucked between her knees, her head hanging down. Her hair was longer than I'd ever seen it, unbraided and unbrushed.

"What is this?" I asked, voice almost a squeak as I made an effort not to shout. "Where? When?"

Amalia didn't take her eyes off the bowl and said simply, "Gehenna."

Confused, I said, "But I thought you couldn't—"

"We can't," Bella interrupted. *"She* can."

"I don't understand."

On the surface of the water, a long shadow stretched across the floor to touch my mother. Whoever was there stayed out of our line of sight.

My mom lifted her face. Tears streamed down her

cheeks, making shiny lines there. "Please," she said. "I'll do anything you want."

"Mom," I breathed, my heart breaking. To Amalia, I insisted, "Is this real?"

Amalia said, "It is."

Bella was breathing in irregular pants. She said, "Her soul is still trapped."

"Trapped?" I asked. "What do you mean?"

Amalia made a small unintelligible sound, then turned to face me. The image in the bowl was snuffed out like a light. "Now you know," she said, and she reached for Ivy.

I let her take the baby, my mind reeling. *Now I know what?* I thought. I didn't know what I knew. I didn't understand. "Is she alive?" I asked, barely daring to hope.

Amalia stood with the baby in her arms, not answering.

I reached out and took a handful of her skirt. "Is she alive?" An edge of hysteria had crept into my voice.

Amalia's spidery fingers brushed over my hand, and I released her. She stepped away. "I will bring Ivy back to you when the time is right," she said, already moving toward the front door.

"Oh my god!" I cried, surging to my feet. "Are you kidding me? This is... This is... insane!"

I felt Bella move up beside me. "I'll explain," she said.

Amalia paused halfway to the door. "You know what has to be done," she said, then continued to the door.

I scrambled toward her, trying to get around the furniture and Bella. Bella blocked my way.

"Don't," Bella said. "She did what she came to do. Let her go."

I met Bella's steady gaze, saw her no-nonsense expression, and I was reminded that she was the p-doc who had informed me when Colin tried to jump off the Malum Center roof. She had a hard core, Dr. Bella Rosenblum did, and—as I would come to understand—it was hardest when she was protecting those she loved.

The front door closed.

First, I felt a void where Ivy's tiny body had been, and then I became aware that my shirt was still unbuttoned. I wasn't embarrassed or ashamed. I was just aware.

"Sit down, Viviane," Bella commanded, her tone forbidding any argument. "I'll make us some tea." She waited until I was seated, then headed for the kitchen.

I got up and ran to the front door. I opened it to the sun shining directly in my face, blinding me. It was a shock to the system, and I cringed away from it. Several long seconds passed before my eyes adjusted.

Amalia was gone.

At my shoulder, invisible Simon said, "Nobody exits stage left like Madam Amalia."

I put all my frustration into one word, "Fuck!"

"Don't worry, Viv," Simon said. "You'll figure something out—probably."

CHAPTER 5

By the time Bella returned with two steaming mugs of tea, I'd found my way back to the couch, gathered my wits, and buttoned my blouse. My breasts had returned to normal—more or less—though Ivy's absence was a new ache.

Amalia's surreal bubble dissipated. It was always like that whenever she was around, as if she knew things no one else did—or at least, that *I* didn't. Big, important things. Like the fact that my mother was still alive. It made no sense. I'd seen her body. I wasn't the only one who had. Hell, we'd buried her.

"Explain it to me," I said to Bella, watching her set the mugs on the coffee table. "What the fuck just happened?"

Bella glanced sideways at me, and for a moment I thought she was going to scold me for cursing. Instead, she said, "What you saw…" She settled down on the couch beside me. "What you saw was your mother's soul. Her body did die that day. You weren't wrong about that."

"Her soul?"

"Her anima. Her atman. Her spirit. The enduring part of her. The eternal part that reincarnates. All living beings have one, but the souls of magickal beings play by different rules. You might say they're more solid—more resilient."

I shifted to face her. "Where is she?"

"In Gehenna." Bella wore sadness like a weighted cloak. It added years to her face. "It's where she's been all this time. It's the reason for her illness. Your father... imprisoned her there."

I wouldn't have been more surprised if I'd fallen off the couch. A proverbial void opened up beneath me, and my entire sense of reality shifted. "What?" I held my breath.

Bella swallowed and licked her lips. "You were young when it happened. Fortunately, he didn't find you. He did, however, find my girl. We'd already been in hiding by then, but he had a power over her that she couldn't resist. I suspect they were communicating through their minds. She thought she could stay hidden from him. She thought he loved her, and maybe he did."

"He found her," I said.

"Yes." Bella's voice grew so quiet I had to lean forward to hear her. "And he... He kept her soul from returning to her body. He locked her away in Gehenna where I couldn't get to her."

"Oh my god," I said. "Her illness?"

"It was because there was no one at home in her

body. Not most of the time, anyway. Occasionally, she could reconnect, but only partially and only for short periods. She never made it all the way back—no matter what I tried."

I remembered those times when she'd been present, when I'd thought it was the curtains of her illness parting, allowing me to see her in her eyes, allowing her to see me. Those precious moments.

"Why didn't you tell me?" I asked.

"It would only have made you more unhappy." Bella wrung her hands. "You couldn't have saved her. I couldn't save her."

Gehenna, I realized, was the source of all my unhappiness. I asked, "So does this mean she's still trapped there? A prisoner?"

"Yes. I had hoped that with her physical death, her spirit would be freed. That..." Bella's voice broke. Tears welled in her eyes. "I was wrong."

"Why? Why did he do this?" I didn't even know my father—the man my mother called Chance—but I already hated him.

"He wanted you."

"Me?" I connected the dots. I was the key to unlocking the doors of Apfallon. He'd taken my mother to blackmail my grandmother. "But you refused to turn me over."

"Of course I refused. Your mother sacrificed everything to keep you safe. I did what I could to keep you hidden."

"The wards at Abram's?" I'd assumed my mother had put them there to protect us.

"And at the Center. I moved your mother into the Center so he wouldn't find her body."

I reeled again. "I should never have brought her here. Was he the one who…"

"I don't know," Bella said quickly. "Maybe."

My insides melted and churned.

Bella put a hand on my forearm. "Don't blame yourself. You're just one small bone in a gigantic monster."

"Rio," I said.

"Yes. Her true name is Ríoghain of the Morrigans." Bella nodded. She pronounced it like "REE-awn" rather than like the city in Brazil. It sounded exotic coming from her.

"She's the one who tricked me into breaking the curse."

"I know the story," Bella said.

"Do you think maybe she killed Mom? Mom's body, I mean?"

Bella shrugged. "I wouldn't put it past her. If your mom knew what she was up to, Rio might do it to keep her quiet. Rio and Chance may have been working together."

Rio had been planning her assault on Apfallon since before I was born. Once she found out that Mom occasionally surfaced, she would have done anything to keep her from spoiling the plot.

"The question now," I said, "is whether she planned it all or my father did."

"Does it matter?" Bella sounded exhausted.

"It matters to me." I sat back, gaze on the fire dying in the fireplace. "All this, and for what? So they can live in Apfallon? It's too much. It's overkill."

"You have to understand," Bella said, "that to the Fomor, this is an uprising. They see themselves as victims of persecution and slavery. This is not just a boundary dispute."

"Are you defending them?"

"No. All I'm saying is that the politics are complicated and personal to both sides."

"Politics," I murmured. "Maybe that's the problem. They've all been approaching this with outdated perspectives. This is the twenty-first century, for god's sake." That's when the seed of my plan germinated. I announced, "We need a treaty. A diplomatic alliance."

In my mind, I added, *And then we can get Mom out of there.*

Jake, Bella, Mr. Jorgenson, and I sat together in the haven's office. It had the hallmarks of Jake's personality and was definitely *his* space. Mid-century furniture in shades of brown gave it an old-fashioned yet stylish atmosphere, and martinis would have been the perfect drink to complement the decor.

"Have you lost your mind?" Jake asked me, winning the award for most ironic statement of the year. "You can't just waltz into Gehenna and ask them to consider a truce with Apfallon. This isn't Israel."

"Actually," I countered, "it kind of is."

"Look," said Jake, his tone dropping into psychologist lecture mode. "Gehenna isn't like other pocket realms. It has a purpose. When you die, your soul goes there to await judgment."

I grimaced, "Judgment? What is this? Bible school?"

Jake waved his hands. "No, okay. Maybe 'judgment' was the wrong word. It's more like 'sorting.'"

I put a purposefully blank expression on my face and asked, "So they put a hat on your head, and it tells you which house you're going to be in?"

Mr. Jorgenson had the cajones to chuckle, and I liked him a little bit more.

"No," Jake said, throwing Mr. Jorgenson a scowl. "It's complicated."

Bella explained, "When magickal beings die, they have to wait to reincarnate until the right time, pre-ordained by the Fates. While they're waiting, they remain in Gehenna. When Normals die, they also go to Gehenna to wait their turn, but for them, it's different. They carry their baggage with them and suffer more."

I squinted around the room. "What you're telling me is that Gehenna is Purgatory?"

"Yes!" Jake exclaimed.

"And the Fomor are the guards," Bella added.

"Wow," I said. "No wonder they want out."

Mr. Jorgenson leaned forward, his large hands expressive. "That's the problem, isn't it? Nobody else wants that job. If the Fomor get back to Apfallon, there'll be nobody minding the inmates."

"I get it," I said. "The Thu are afraid of that. But you can't force people just because you're afraid no one else will do the job. It's wrong. We need a better system."

"Nobody likes change," Jake said mournfully.

Bella noted, "Change is already on its way. The Fomor have breached Apfallon."

"If I can get both sides to the table," I said, "I'm sure we can find a better way. Together. I need to get to Gehenna." Admittedly, my agenda was two-fold. I honestly did hope to get the Fomor into negotiations with the Thu, but I also wanted desperately to see my mom.

"You can't go into Gehenna," Jake said. "You're alive."

"My mom was alive, and she got in."

"She had a Fomor drag her in."

I stared at him. "Did you know about that?"

Pressing his palms flat on his desk, Jake said, "Not exactly. Not until recently."

"And *you* didn't tell me either." My frustration was showing.

Bella spoke up. "Maybe Colin could get her there?"

The suggestion didn't please Jake, but I saw it as a ray of hope—okay, a small spark of hope.

"I thought Colin was ostracized," Jake said.

Bella nodded.

It was true. Colin had run away from Gehenna and his family. He'd been branded a traitor, or at least, that's what I was led to believe. I said, "That may have been part of Rio's ruse."

Once again, my mind presented the idea that Colin had conspired with Rio—been in on it the whole time. It made me physically ill, and I shoved the thought away. Facing Bella, I said, "I need to talk to him. Do you know where he is?"

Bella gave me a worried look. "I haven't spoken with him since you broke the curse."

I'd been trying to jump the moon to him ever since

I'd woken up in Apfallon—to no avail. Not even after I'd returned to the haven. I said, "I haven't been able to reach him with my magick."

"That won't work if he's in Gehenna," Bella said. "For the same reason I can't scry there."

Mr. Jorgenson jumped in, "Practically speaking, you should get the Thu on board with your plan before you go to Gehenna. If you don't, you'll just be making empty promises to the Fomor. I know Lady Gliton, and she doesn't want this war. You have a better chance of getting *her* to agree to negotiate. Start there."

I wanted to say, "But my Mom!" but I didn't. I had to take this one step at a time if I wanted to succeed. Mr. Jorgenson was right, and suddenly I had a plan of action. Lenore, Colin, and then Mom. In that order. One step at a time.

CHAPTER 6

Corona was on a high the next morning, having discovered that Simon was back. She burst into my room shortly *after* dawn and woke me by bouncing on my bed.

I'd spent a mostly sleepless night trying to telepathically contact Colin—to no avail. When I'd finally given up, shortly *before* dawn, I'd slept. Until...Corona.

"Viv, Viv, Viv," she chanted. "Simon's back."

"I know," I said, groggy.

Corona settled in next to me, her head beside mine on the pillow. She lowered her voice to a whisper. "He says there's going to be a war."

"Not if I can help it," I told her, opening my eyes to slits.

"You can stop it?"

"I'm going to try."

"That's good. 'Cause the Lamby-kins are all freaking out."

"The who?"

"You know." She tapped a finger with each name. "Jake and Mr. Jorgenson and Ayu and Booker and Hilda and Jamal. Oh, and Carrie. The Lost Lambs team."

"I see."

"So, are you going to fight the Fomor?"

"What?" I closed my eyes again. "No. I'm going to get them to sign a treaty."

Corona said nothing, but I could feel her staring at me.

I asked, "What?"

She sighed.

"Corona?" I asked. "What's wrong?"

She whispered, "You probably won't let me help you."

I opened one eye. "Why would you say that?"

"'Cuz…"

"'Cuz why?"

"'Cuz you didn't let me help with that Agate girl. You just took off." Corona rolled over on her back so she could cross her arms angrily on her chest.

I sighed. "And you're bringing this up now because…"

"Because I want to help this time." She rolled back to face me, earnest. "When we were at the Center, I was Lady Gisèle's handmaiden. I helped keep her safe—until I didn't." Her bottom lip pushed out in a pout. "And now, I can be yours. I know stuff. I have skills."

"I don't doubt it, but this could be dangerous."

"So? I helped you kill the hag, remember? And I

fought off that stupid selkie who tried to drown me."

I moved my arm up under my pillow and opened both eyes fully. "You're pretty brave," I said.

"Damn straight, I am." She sat up, cross-legged and facing me. Her hands danced like butterflies as she talked, fluttering, flitting from thought flower to thought flower. "Here's what I think," she said. "We need to get you into Apfallon first, right? But it's locked down. No one in or out."

"How do you know that?"

"Simon, of course."

"Where *is* Simon this morning?"

"Doesn't matter." She waved the question off. "Are you able to jump the moon to Lady Lenore?"

I shook my head. "Not when she's in Apfallon. I tried last night. No connection. It's okay, though. I might be able to get a message to her. She owns the bookstore, and I know where she lives. Someone's got to know how to reach her, right?"

"Maybe." Corona tapped her chin, pondering, then said, "Unless they're all in Apfallon too, but we can cross that troll bridge when we come to it. What are you going to do once you get to Apfallon?"

"Convince Lenore to host peace talks."

"Straightforward. K.I.S.S. I like it."

"K.I.S.S?"

"Keep it simple, stupid. Kind of like Occam's razor. The simplest solution is often the right one. Simon says we don't have much time though, so we better get a move on." She made to roll away, then stopped and dug in her jeans pocket. "Oh. I forgot. You should see this."

Corona produced a folded piece of paper. She opened it and turned it to face me. It was a wanted poster with a rather accurate drawing of me in the middle, and it said, "Wanted for crimes against Apfallon. Viviane Rose." It had been photocopied a little crooked, and at the bottom—added in blue marker and jagged handwriting—were the words, "Dead or alive."

I gasped. "Is this a joke?"

"A little," Corona said. "But not. It's not official. There are just lots of kith who blame you for what's happening. It's a grassroots movement."

"I see." I sat up. "I guess that means we better be careful."

"Things are messed up in Wyrdwood," Corona said. "People are pissed."

I climbed out of bed. "They can join the freakin' club."

I dressed for anonymity. I wasn't having a good hair day anyway—more dishwater blond and flat than usual. I found an old baseball cap in the hall closet and tucked my hair up under it. Jeans, a black turtleneck to keep back the Autumn chill, and my red coat. The coat wasn't exactly subtle, but I hadn't yet worn it in Wyrdwood. I felt secure in my secret identity.

Corona wore jeans and a yellow button-down shirt. She'd found an old khaki trenchcoat that was two sizes too big for her. It hung almost to her ankles, and she could cross-wrap herself in it. She didn't wear a hat, but she did wet her hair and slick it down. As it dried, of course, it didn't take long for it to revert to its original chaos.

Simon joined us with his usual abruptness. "Good morning, ladies," he said out of nowhere. When I looked toward his voice, the vague outline of his goldfish body began to appear. "Oh no, you don't," he said to me. "I'm incognito today. No lookin' at me with your Sight, yeah?"

I agreed, though it was hard not to look at him, especially once we were in the car. Seeing a gold fish floating around in the back seat was too distracting.

We took one of the haven vehicles. I drove us down the ridge and into Wyrdwood. As we entered the Old Towne on Main Street, I felt the hackles go up on the back of my neck. I couldn't put my finger on why. Aside from the Halloween decorations everywhere, nothing seemed out of place. Pedestrians walked along the sidewalks, in and out of shops, and across at the crosswalks, just as they had every other time I'd been down there. Something was amiss though.

"Feel that?" asked Simon. "Antici...pation."

I asked, "What do you mean?"

"Wyrdwood's holding its breath. Waiting for the other shoe to drop."

"I feel it," Corona said quietly.

I watched an Orcneas woman with a stocky child hurry down the street. "Are they worried violence will spill into Wyrdwood?"

"Aye." Simon's voice was thoughtful. "No one knows what'll happen. Many have friends or family in Apfallon. Others worry about an influx of refugees. Still others think the Fomor won't stop at Apfallon. I guarantee it's the main topic of discussion at every supper table around town."

We said nothing more until we arrived in front of Lenore's Wyrdwood home. The small house looked even more adorable in the daylight. The leaves of the Japanese maples were falling, painting the lawn in shades of red, and the roses had died on their bushes, rose hips hanging heavy in their places. A pair of jack-o-lanterns sat on either side of the front door, their eyes dark and empty.

Before we were all out of the car, the front door

opened, and Kushala stepped out. She looked fragile—moreso than usual. Her short, gray afro was pulled into tiny nubs all over her head, and she had wrapped herself in an evergreen shawl to keep back the cool air. The last time I'd seen her had been just after my mother's funeral when Abram and I had come for dinner with her and Lenore. I didn't remember her having those dark circles under her eyes back then.

We trudged up the walk to her. I said, "Hi, Kushala."

She acknowledged me with a nod, then said, "You don't need to come any further."

Corona and I halted in place.

"I want to—" I began.

Kushala interrupted me. "I knew you were coming," she said. "I know what you want." The green of her shawl enhanced the emerald of her eyes. "I can't help you. She wouldn't let me go back with her."

I said, "She wants you to be safe."

"She doesn't want me to watch her die."

My heart ached. "I need to talk to her," I said. "I think I can negotiate a treaty."

Kushala's head flew back, and she laughed. It was a raw and emotional sound, driven less by humor than cynicism. "Wide-eyed child. So gullible, even after all that's been done to you. The door is open, and once opened, it cannot be closed again. The monsters are inside."

I took a step toward her, palms up. "There has to be a way. I have to try. This is all my fault."

Eyelids half closed, she stared down her nose at me. "Yes," she said. "It is. And yet, it isn't. No one in House Gliton blames you. We are well aware of how spectacularly we failed you."

I sighed. I wasn't about to argue with her about whose fault it was. I just wanted to fix it. I said, "Please, Kushala. Please. There must be a way to reach her. Can I send her a message? Surely there's a way?"

"You can walk away," the elderly woman said. "Never look back, and never know the worst of it. You can live your life. No one will blame you."

"No one but me," I replied. "I know I'm new to all this, but it's my family. My mom. My grandmother and my great-grandmother. If you won't help me, then I'll find another way. I'm not giving up, Kushala. I'm not."

Corona added, "Yeah!"

Kushala said nothing, watching me with those piercing eyes.

Finally, I said, "Family," one last time, and she caved.

"Lenore will divorce me for telling you this," Kushala said, "and I can't guarantee your safety."

"I don't care about my safety. What is it?"

"The bookstore is closed, and I don't have a key, but there's a portal inside. You can't tell anyone, and make sure you're not followed or observed. You'll have to figure out a way to get by Lenore's security. I have no idea what obstacles you'll face if you break in, but the portal's in the back, behind a stack of boxes. Tell the boxes that Abraham Lincoln sent you, and they'll move aside. Then you can pass through into Apfallon."

"The boxes will move?" I asked, incredulous.

"That's what I said."

"All righty. Thank you!" I put my palms together and gestured my gratitude. "C'mon, Corona. Let's go." I headed back toward the car.

Kushala called out, "Tell her I love her, and I'm waiting."

"I will," I replied, opening the car door. "I'll tell her."

CHAPTER 7

Downtown Wyrdwood had a strange vibe. I parked the car as close to the "Prose, Poetry, & Poe" book shop as I could, and we got out onto the sidewalk. The buildings in that part of town were old-fashioned, medieval even, and resembled a European village more than an American one. Once more, I was struck by how quaint it was. Well-kept, certainly, but more like Epcot than Normal, USA. It may as well have been pulled—whole cloth—out of history and dropped onto the coast of Oregon. Only the small accoutrements on the buildings—the electric street lights, the neon signs in shops, the phone lines stretched between structures, and the products in the stores—gave away that we hadn't stepped into a different time and place. I loved it.

And then there were the inhabitants. I could only imagine how Wyrdwood appeared to Normals. Many of the residents of Wyrdwood were anything but normal. I recognized a few races, though not all. Some were of mixed race, and that made it harder to identify ancestry. Others were foreign enough that I wasn't familiar with them.

Jake had told me that the mythologies of our world were actually true. All of them. From Nordic to Christian, from Japanese to Hindu, from Buddhist to Jewish—Maori, Russian, Mbuti... Arabic, Aztec, Apache, Armenian. All of it. The races, the heroes, the evil, and even the gods were all real—at one point. Many had offspring, and their offspring had offspring. Reincarnation played a mysterious role as well.

It came down to those with magickal blood—the kith—and those without—Normals. Anyone with magickal blood could see the true forms of the kith. Normals were prevented from the Sight except with special dispensation provided by a spell or curse. Over the centuries, millennia even, the kith bred with Normals, mingling the blood.

I was of mixed race ancestry. I had magickal blood but I looked as Normal as my grandfather—who had none. I had a surface understanding of it all, having only just discovered my truth within the past few months. I was still a newbie when it came to Wyrdwood.

I hadn't spent much time in town, but that day, I could tell the energy was off. Pedestrians on the street moved quickly, many with their heads down. They weren't strolling as I'd seen them do in the past. Most were talking on their cellphones or checking their watches as if they were all late for a meeting I hadn't been invited to. If any were Normals going about their business, they too had picked up on the tension in the air and were mimicking the same uneasy behavior.

On our way to the bookstore, Corona and I tried to remain unnoticed, pausing to window-shop if anyone passed too close. I felt ridiculous, but Simon's paranoid warnings kept me in check.

"Don't let them see your face," he'd warned more than once.

We paused at the crosswalk, waiting for the light to change. I caught the eye of a man with a beard that nearly covered his whole face. Only the reddened tip of his nose and the rounded tops of his cheeks stood out from the bushy brown nest. He studied me with dispassion for a moment, then his eyes widened and his eyebrows raised.

Too late, I ducked to one side, hiding my face. He'd recognized me.

I waited for the fall-out, but all he did was jay-walk across the street so he wouldn't have to cross paths with us. I was relieved.

We made it to Lenore's shop without incident, only to confirm that the front door was locked, and the interior was dark. The shop had a Tudor-style façade with criss-crossing beams and white-washed bricks between them. In its bay windows, it showcased books with creative and attractive displays. I got sucked into real window-shopping and mental wish-list creating.

Corona sheltered her eyes with her hands and put

her nose to the glass. "How do we get in?"

Simon piped up. "Y'don't want to stay on the street too long."

"Oh c'mon," I grumbled. "It's not that bad. No-body's going to shoot me or anything."

"Hmph," Simon grunted. "They could do worse."

"I'm gonna go down the alley," Corona said. "See what's back there."

I nodded. "Good idea. We can all go."

An alley ran along one side of the shop, narrow and paved with uneven cobblestones. The walls closed in on either side and the overhanging roofs restricted the sun-light. Trash cans and dumpsters lined the edge, and the smell coming from them was rancid.

"Ew, gross," Corona said, stepping over the corpse of a rat.

A rickety old fire escape clung desperately to the side of the building there, and we found the shop's back door. Corona tried it, but it was also locked.

I knocked. "Hello? Anyone in there?"

"Who d'ye think is going to answer?" Simon asked.

"I don't know," I replied. "The security guard, may-be?"

No one answered.

"What about that window?" Corona asked.

Next to the alley door, a window of paned glass sat

high on the wall.

Simon's voice came from near it. "It's dark inside. But it looks like the window's unlatched. It opens out. If you can get up here, you could get in."

"What about you?" I asked. "Why don't you float up there, go in, and unlock the door from inside?"

Simon's tone turned sarcastic. "Gaw! Thanks for pointing out that I have no hands. Hell of a friend you are."

"You open doors all the time!"

"Sure. Normal doors. This one's warded against magick."

"Fine," I said.

The bottom of the window was about eight feet off the ground. I could reach it with my fingertips—just barely—if I stretched, but I wouldn't be able to pull myself up. I searched for an idea. The dumpster caught my eye. "Help me move this over there," I said.

Simon warned, "It'll make a racket."

"We'll go slowly." It wasn't going to be easy, rolling it across cobblestones, but it was our best shot. "Simon, go keep a look-out. If anyone's coming, let us know."

"Aye. I'd rather not go into Apfallon anyway. I'll wait here for ye to come back."

Corona sounded disappointed as she said, "You don't want to come with us?"

"I'm not exactly Lenore's favorite person right now," Simon said.

"Why not?" Corona asked.

Simon made a bubble-bursting sound, presumably with his mouth. He said, "Ye're running out of time. Ye'd best go on your own. I'll be here when ye come out. Just be careful."

"We will," I promised.

Corona and I positioned ourselves behind the dumpster and pushed. It moved in fits and chunks, but we made steady progress. Fortunately, it was nearly empty, so it wasn't as heavy as it could've been.

Once we got it under the window, I climbed up to sit on the edge of the lid. "I don't think we should step on the lid," I told Corona. "It doesn't look strong enough to hold us." With one hand on the wall, I inched up to my feet, standing on the lip. It was the perfect height to reach the window.

A latch on the inside of the window was undone, and I hooked my nails into the wood of the frame and pulled. At first, it resisted, but on the second try, it gave way, and the window swung wide. A gust of warm air escaped from the opening.

"I'm going in," I told Corona. "Keep a look-out."

"I got your six, man," Corona said.

I hauled myself in through the window and ended

up in a bathroom. It looked more utilitarian than decorated. That was a relief. The window was high on the wall, so I had to lower myself inside, using the toilet as a step ladder. The aroma of cinnamon was thick, coming from a solid air freshener that I accidentally knocked off the toilet tank as I descended. It hit the floor with a clatter.

I went to the bathroom door and opened it. The bookstore was a series of shelf units all stocked with books. The overhead lights were off, and the only illumination came in through bay windows at the front. Thick shadow obscured the area in the back.

I stood on the toilet seat again and stuck my head back out the window. "You coming?"

Corona climbed in more nimbly than I had, and soon we were heading out into the store.

The bookshelves dampened all sound, even our footfalls, and I unconsciously kept my voice low. "Kushala said the portal was in the back," I said.

"Right," Corona whispered back. "Behind a magickal stack of boxes."

We headed deeper in, and I wished we'd thought to bring a flashlight. As if reading my mind, Corona pulled out her cellphone and turned on the flashlight app. I smiled at her and did the same.

We reached the last row of shelves where a door on

the back wall stood ajar.

"Ow!" cried Corona.

"You okay?" I asked, then a sudden intense pain lit up the back of my shoulder. I cried out in surprise.

"OW!" Corona was dancing around, swatting.

My butt sparked with pain as if someone had pinched me. I heard a fluttering buzz, like a humming-bird or large bee.

And then, something flew up in front of my nose, hovered there, and stared me down. It was the strangest creature I'd ever seen. About eight inches tall, it was a tiny person with dragonfly wings and a chameleon-like tail that curled forward between its legs. Its hair was dark and thick, including its mustache, beard, and body hair. It wore no clothes, had a round belly, buff limbs, and a tiny—albeit impressive in relation to the creature's overall size—penis.

It looked me in the eyes, then called out in a deep voice, "She sees me!"

A chorus of ahhs and uhhhhs went up around the room, and then the macho fairy-thing punched my nose—hard. It made tears rise into my eyes, and I cried out again.

"Get out!" the creature shouted, leaning forward, arms back, putting its all into the command.

A pinch to my other butt cheek made me jump and

put my hand back to protect myself.

"They're all around us," Corona said, squirming to keep away from their strong little fingers. She slapped at one that flew too close, but it was far too agile to get struck.

"We can't," I said. "We need to... Ow! Stop it!" I looked frantically around myself, trying to avoid their attacks. "We need to get to Apfallon."

"Apfallon is closed," replied the hairy one.

Corona growled.

"Listen, fairy man," I said. "We don't want any trouble. Just let us through. I'm going there to speak with Lenore. I'm her great-granddaughter!"

"Liar!" accused the creature. "If you were a Gliton, you'd know that I. Am. Not. A. Fairy! I'm a fucking pixie!"

"Okay, okay. Sorry."

A trickle of blood ran down Corona's face from where one of the pixies had broken the skin at her hairline.

"Listen, you little assholes," I said, my frustration overpowering my diplomacy. "Can we just talk for a minute? Please? I can explain!" One of the creatures was tangled in Corona's hair. Another had crawled up inside my coat and was getting dangerously close to bare skin.

The hairy pixie glared at me a moment longer, then

put two fingers in his mouth and whistled. "Cease fire!" he bellowed.

"Thank you," I said, and I felt the pixie in my coat go still. It didn't leave, but at least it wasn't invading any deeper.

Corona stopped spinning in place and focused on trying to extricate the pixie from her hair. Her cheeks were flushed.

The pixie crossed his arms on his chest, his biceps bulging. "You got thirty seconds," he said. "Why shouldn't we tear you apart? 'Cuz we could, you know? Like a chicken in a school of piranhas." He clacked his teeth together as if biting, and I didn't doubt him for a second.

I took a breath, calming down ever so slightly. "My name is Viviane Rose, and I want to stop this war with the Fomor before it—"

"You're Viviane Rose?" The pixie's eyes narrowed. "You're the one who tricked our lady into breaking the curse?"

Corona mumbled, "Oh, shit."

I put my hands up. "Yes, but I didn't do it on purpose. I was tricked too. I was stabbed! I was...dying. Look, I just want to fix things!"

The pixie inside my coat repositioned itself. Its presence there was an odd combination of warm intimacy and disturbing invasion of privacy.

"Twenty seconds," growled the hairy pixie.

I talked fast, "I've lived my whole life among Normals. I didn't know any of this existed, not Wyrdwood, not Apfallon—"

"Not Orcneas nor Selkies," added Corona.

I continued, "I was tricked, but now I think I have a way to make it all right again. The last thing I want is for anyone to die because of me. I just need to speak to Lenore and tell her my plan. She'll want to see me. I promise!"

"Ten." The hairy pixie cracked his knuckles. "If that was true, she'd have told us to bring you. But no, she's too busy figuring out how to keep the Fomor from slaughtering our friends and families."

"She doesn't know I'm coming. But..."

"Seven."

"At least send someone to tell her I'm here. See if she won't see me."

"Four."

"I can pay you."

"Three."

"Please. I'm begging you. This is a matter of life or death."

"Yeah, yours," huffed another of the pixies, somewhere at my back.

The hairy pixie flexed, making fists of his little hands. "Not good enough," he said. "Get 'em!"

The pixies attacked en masse, and I was assaulted with bites and pinches all over. Any exposed skin was especially vulnerable. They pulled my hair and my eyebrows. They bit my earlobes and the backs of my hands. The one inside my coat found some skin at my waist and sunk its teeth into me.

Overwhelmed and in pain, bleeding from numerous small wounds, I scrambled to get away, but I couldn't escape them. I tried picking them off, my hand closing around their bodies, limbs or even heads before I flung them away. They always came back.

When Corona fell to the floor and curled into a fetal position, crying, I'd had enough. I put my hands out, summoned all my willpower, and shouted, "Get off us!" Magick flowed out through my fingertips and surrounded me like an aura. The pixies attached to me were blown back. The one inside my coat went still.

All around me, pixies fell to the floor—male and female pixies of varying ages, skin tones, and hair styles, all naked, all with dragonfly wings and chameleon tails.

I glared down at them as they picked themselves up. "Stay down."

They obeyed. Not a one flew up into the air. Most rolled to stand, rubbing their heads, elbows, or butts.

They fluttered out their wings and checked themselves—and each other—for injuries.

I said, tone commanding, "I'm going to Apfallon whether you like it or not. I don't want to hurt you, but I will if you try to stop me." My fingers tingled with magick.

The pixies crawled into small groups and clung to one another, whispering.

"Wow," said Corona, getting slowly to her feet. She was a mess of torn clothes and blood stains.

"You okay?" I asked her.

"Yeah, though narrowly escaping 'Death by a Thousand Bites' is not my favorite way to spend the day."

I unbuttoned my coat. My shirt was stained with blood. I reached in, took hold of the pixie that had infiltrated my clothing, and pulled her out by her foot. I held her up, letting her dangle a moment. She twisted and writhed. Her tiny face showed her fear. I lay her gently onto the palm of my other hand. "I'm on your side," I told her.

Her long red hair kept falling across her eyes and catching in her mouth. She tried to push it back so she could keep me in her sights. She crawled to the edge of my hand and dove off, taking flight halfway down and zipping away.

The hairy pixie walked forward then flew up into the air so we were face-to-face again. "I hate you," he said. "For what you did."

"I'm sorry," I told him with abundant sincerity.

He grunted, put his hands on his hips, and looked down toward the floor as if in thought.

I was trying hard to look anywhere but at his tiny genitals.

"You can go," he said finally. "I'll escort you in, and if you're not telling the truth, I'll kill you. Capiche?"

I nodded. "I understand."

"Only you." He nodded at me. "Not your body-guard."

Corona protested. "Oh no. Where she goes, I go."

The pixie lifted his hefty eyebrows at me and waited for my response.

I faced Corona and said, "Someone should tell Jake what's happening. If we both just disappear, then they'll worry. I won't be long. Soon as I'm back, I'll come find you."

Corona pouted but didn't object. She nodded. "Okay. Good luck."

I said, "All right, fairy man—"

"Pixie!"

"Sorry. Pixie. Lead the way."

"Name's Apollo." The pixie turned and flew toward the back room. The other pixies quickly took to the air and zipped out of my way as I made to follow him. I felt around on my scalp and my fingers came away stained with blood. I had sore spots all over, including on my shoulders and legs, and I suspected I looked like I'd been hit by a shrapnel grenade.

"You guys are pretty badass," I said.

"Don't ever forget it." Apollo threw a grin over his shoulder. It changed his entire demeanor, and I found myself smiling back. He said, "Abraham Lincoln sent us," and boxes slid aside.

CHAPTER 8

The bookstore portal led to the main room in a wood cabin. It looked like the kind of place my grandfather would rent for vacation—taxidermied birds, fish, and deer heads on the walls, and a large fireplace with overstuffed furniture designed for napping or reading. Golden sunlight shone in through the windows.

"Wait here," the pixie commanded. "I'd better announce you—for your own safety. And clean yourself up. Bathroom, that way. Take some clothes from the hall closet."

"Um, sure," I replied, looking in the direction he indicated.

Apollo flew straight at the window. For a moment, I was afraid he didn't see the glass, but then he waggled his tiny fingers, and the window unlatched and opened just wide enough for him to get out.

My world had certainly changed, and I was surprised by how easily I seemed to be adjusting. One might say it was as if I'd been born for it. Either that, or I was due for a breakdown in my near future.

When I saw myself in the bathroom mirror, I gasped. I looked worse than Corona had, with blood smeared on my forehead, drying in my hair and on my cheeks, and small inflamed wounds all over. I looked like I'd been attacked by a swarm of wasps.

The bathroom had contemporary facilities. It seemed modern plumbing was valued even in Apfallon. In the hall closet, I found piles of clothing in all sizes—pants, shirts, skirts, socks, and even underwear. I undressed and decided to just hop into the shower rather than try to take a cat bath. The towels and washcloths were luxurious, and I found bandages in the cabinet for the worst of my wounds. They had all stopped bleeding, thank goodness.

I dressed in loose-fitting pants and a blouse that was a size too big for me—all in chocolate brown linen. The clothes I'd been wearing were ruined, torn and stained, so I shoved them into the bathroom's garbage can. By the time I was done, I felt much calmer.

I wandered back into the living room, browsing its contents. An array of knick-knacks on the mantelpiece caught my eye. They were an assortment of skulls—bird, mouse, mole, cat, and human-shaped skulls of varying sizes from a few inches across to one that Hamlet might have dug up. Works of art, they all had elaborate designs carved into their surfaces.

I found it hard to imagine Lenore keeping them or decorating her space with dead animals.

"Who are you?" came a deep, gruff voice with a slight Scandinavian accent.

I turned toward it to find a short man—and by short, I mean four feet tall—with a thick beard and squinty eyes. His body was stocky, his muscles abundant. He wore a brown corduroy field jacket and relaxed jeans, and he casually carried a large handgun—a blunderbuss with a flared muzzle. Though he wasn't pointing it at me, the warning was clear.

"I'm waiting to see Lenore," I said. "I'm—"

"That's Lady Lenore, if you please," the man corrected me. "Or Madame Lenore. Or Mistress Lenore."

"Okay, sorry." I felt the uncanny urge to curtsy but just nodded instead.

The man eyed me. "Who are you?"

"Viviane Rose. I'm Len...Lady Lenore's great-granddaughter."

The man's jaw tightened, and—though I wouldn't have thought it possible—his eyes hardened even more. "*The* Viviane Rose?" he asked.

I nodded, less sure of myself. "It was an accident," I offered. "I was tricked."

His upper lip curled enough that I could see it despite his shaggy mustache. "I'm Gore. The Gliton gamekeeper. I presume you came through the portal?"

"I have an escort. A pixie. Apollo," I said, hoping

that would ease the tension in the room. "He went to announce me to...L-Lady Lenore."

"Hm," grunted Gore. He crossed his arms, cradling his gun in the crook of his elbow, and watched me.

The silence stretched. I shifted my weight from one foot to the other. Eventually, I had to say something. I glanced around at the room. "Nice place," I said.

Gore huffed a laugh as if I were the most predictable idiot he'd ever encountered. Then nothing.

I cast around for a new topic. "Did you carve the skulls?" I asked. "They're amazing."

Gore grunted, but his stance softened just a touch.

I pressed on. "You're very talented. It can't be easy working on bone like that."

To his credit, Gore tried to snub me. I saw his mouth move, his eyes dart, and his weight shift. He fought the urge to talk to me and lost. "The bone determines the design," he said.

"Really?" I encouraged. "What do you mean?"

"I fit the curves and lines to the landscape of the skull," he said.

I knew I had him when he set the gun aside and crossed to the mantlepiece. "Every skull is different," he said. "Sometimes I meditate for days on a skull before the design comes to me."

"Amazing," I said.

"I sleep with it on the pillow next to mine. It gets into my dreams, and the pattern appears fully formed in my consciousness when I wake up."

I wasn't faking interest anymore. "No kidding," I said. "And then you start carving?"

"It's a gift. Been in my family since the beginning of time. If a shepherd's prize ram dies or is killed, I carve the skull and horns—for a fee, of course. The shepherd takes it back home to protect the rest of his flock. It's for luck. For protection." He reached up and ran a finger along the symbols carved into a human skull. "For keeping Death at bay."

"Wow," I said. "And the human one?"

"This is my son's skull. He fell ill, and it consumed him. I carved his skull to keep my other eleven children safe."

"I'm sorry for your loss," I said.

Gore nodded.

"Eleven children?" I perched on the arm of the sofa. "I hope it worked."

Gore rumbled a laugh deep in his belly. "I have a herd of grandchildren to prove it did."

"You don't look old enough to have grandchildren," I told him, buttering him up.

He laughed aloud, a rich and spontaneous sound. "I have great-grandchildren," he said, amusement shining in his eyes. He moved to one of the armchairs and sat down. His small stature made him look like a child himself—albeit a hirsute one.

He sobered and asked, "Why have you come back?"

"To make things right," I said. "Fix what I broke."

He replied, "Those are a hero's words."

"Maybe," I replied. "I have to do something."

"That's where it always begins," Gore said.

At that moment, Apollo zipped in through the open window and hovered between us.

"Gore," said Apollo.

"Apollo," Gore replied.

"You didn't kill her?"

Gore shook his head slowly. "Nope. Figured there was plenty of time for that later."

"True dat," Apollo said. "But right now, Her Lady-ship wants me to take Viviane to the manor."

"Then you'd better go." Gore pushed up from the chair and folded his hands together over his belly. "Miss Rose, you ever think of anything an old dwarf can do to help you with your quest, you come back here." He walked to the mantel and took down a small skull. "This belonged to a guardian owl that used to live in my barn." He carried it to me and held it out. "You're going to need its wisdom and keen eyesight on your journey. The way will get very dark before you reach the light."

I took the skull from him. "Thank you."

"I suggest you find a chain or ribbon for it. Hang it around your neck. It will be less likely to get crushed if you keep it between your breasts."

I blinked. "Oh. Okay. Thanks."

"Now, git. It does no good to keep the lady of the manor waiting."

Apollo waited for me to open the door.

"Nice to have met you, Gore," I said.

"One for the history books," the dwarf replied.

Gliton Manor sat in a shallow valley between evergreen hills. Three small lakes—a triangle, a circle, and a square—reflected the gray clouds overhead. A wide stream connected them and flowed off into the distance in both directions.

A large galleon hovered thirty feet above the ground, anchored in place with thick rope to keep it from drifting. Instead of sails, three hot air balloons kept it aloft. At the front, a figurehead—an elephant man with large ears and a trunk draped over his shoulder—looked out across the land and stretched his arms forward as if to push away all obstacles.

We passed beneath the ship, crossing through its

shadow. The shadow's edge stretched ahead of us as if spreading into a morbid Hollywood red-carpet. Either the ship was sinking, or the sun was. In any case, it gave me a chill. The ship's wood creaked, and I was glad when we finally emerged on the other side.

The manor lay ahead. It was an architectural mish-mash of modular pieces. When I'd seen it last, it had shone like crystal in sunshine. Alive. Light.

No more.

A pall had come over it. The walls had hunkered down, darkened, and become gray. The windows were shuttered, and a wide moat surrounded it where there hadn't been one before. Gliton Manor was preparing for war.

In front of it, troops marched, trained, and worked on equipment—with complete disregard for the garden. They trampled the flower beds and turned the grassy lawn into muddy mulch. Topiary creatures sat among the groups of workers and practicing fighters. An emer-ald dragon scowled at me, its head lowered as if ready-ing to pounce. A pair of mermaids clutched one another, their leaves having dropped enough that the skeleton of their limbs was visible. All the topiary hedges looked rough and ready for a fight.

The troops were a magickal mix of races. I saw centaurs, satyrs, giants, and dwarves like Gore. Elves of the Tolkien variety practiced with bows and arrows, and elves of the Santa variety smelted weapons. Those were the races I could identify—undoubtedly incorrectly. It took my breath away.

The people all wore a mix of attire and armor from different cultures and centuries right up to modern day camo, and some wore little to nothing at all. Once again, I was blown away by Apfallon's diversity. It made my Reality seem bland and restricted in comparison.

Everyone had a task to perform. Children carried baskets and shadowed adults. Swarms of pixies performed complex air maneuvers. Those who weren't practicing their martial arts were crafting and armoring.

It was a Renn Faire without the music, joy, or laughter.

"Keep moving," grunted Apollo, hovering and looking back over his shoulder at me.

I followed him down the slope to where a path cut between two of the lagoons.

When someone spotted me, word spread quickly, and I became the target of unfriendly eyes, words, and gestures.

All work slowed, and a man dressed in a white and turquoise uniform marched around yelling at people to get back to it. It was a losing battle.

"Viviane Rose," they whispered.

"It's her."

"The mistress's great-grandchild."

"The war-starter."

"All her fault."

"Why'd she come back?"

"Traitor."

Apollo flew up to my shoulder and perched there. "Ignore them," he said. "They won't dare touch you. Just keep moving."

The stream had an arched bridge over it, wide enough for a car to drive across. I kept my eyes on it as I advanced. Someone had carved the surface of it with roses and leaves to provide traction and to stream away rainwater. On either side, it had low railings of the same wood, also carved with blooming rose vines.

The troops parted as we walked toward the main entrance. They gave us plenty of space, all watching with grim expressions.

I felt the need to apologize and opened my mouth to say I was sorry.

Apollo pinched my earlobe. "Do not engage," he ordered.

The uniformed man moved down the line, ordering people away. "Get back to work," he shouted over and over, to no avail.

I was relieved to see the double front doors of the

manor house open, and Lenore stepped out with an entourage of guards. She stood there, hands folded in front, expression regal, and waited for me to join her. The years had fallen off her again, and I was struck by how strong she appeared, relative to the doddering old woman I'd first met. She wore her hair in intricate braids that capped her head, and she was dressed in tight-fitting doe-skin breeches and matching vest, knee-high riding boots, a simple white blouse, and an old-fashioned hunting coat with the placket of buttons undone.

Apollo flew up off my shoulder and zoomed ahead. He bowed in mid-air. "Your ladyship," he said.

Lenore replied, "Thank you, Apollo. You may go. I'll send for you when Viviane is ready to return to Reality."

Apollo bowed again, turned to look at me with his eyebrows raised, then flitted off.

I would have hugged Lenore, but she turned away when I got close.

"You'd better come inside," she said. "We can talk there."

I followed her escort inside. Their boots echoed loudly on the marble floor in the foyer.

I hadn't seen that room when I'd stayed at the manor after the stabbing. It was tall and broad, with a curving staircase at the far end. White walls had wainscoting and paintings of fantastic scenes that reminded me of Waterhouse's works—except they pulled no punches nor romanticized the scenes. Each framed work of art had a plaque that named its subject.

"Tanuki." The painting showed a fox-faced man sitting in a Buddha pose before several human petitioners. His expression revealed cunning, and he had testicles so large he could drape them over a frame to keep the rain off himself.

"Naiads." Water nymphs coaxed a child into a lake where another child had already drowned.

"Syrinx." A terrified young woman ran in a panic, chased by Pan, his penis erect, his intent obvious.

"Jvarasura." A radiant man in traditional Tibetan robes wrapped his arms around a woman in the throes of illness, her body sweating, her eyes rolling back in her head, and her mouth open with a cry of anguish.

There were many more, and I could have spent hours examining them all, but a gentle push from behind let me know I should continue forward. Lenore had gone into a side room—a small living room with two couches facing one another around a coffee table. It was surprisingly intimate, unlike other common rooms I'd seen in the manor.

A woman with blue-ish skin and hair, dressed in the kind of suit you'd expect to see on a Man in Black or CIA agent, came out of a second door carrying a tray with a coffee pot and all the fixings. She set it on the coffee table while Lenore took a seat on one of the couches. The server's eyes were large and slanted up at the outer edges, pupils swallowing the iris entirely—black holes in the whites. She served the coffee.

"Please, sit," said Lenore, indicating the couch across from her.

One of the other attendants was already closing the drapes on the windows, but not before I saw people craning to see in.

Lenore said, "They're curious about you. You don't have to worry. They won't hurt you. Not here in Apfallon. Not while I'm alive."

I sat down. "Lenore, I—"

She cut me off with a subtle and regal gesture, then waved her entourage out of the room. Only once they were gone, did she lower her hand. "Now, we can speak. You realize you're risking your life coming here uninvited?"

"I figured that out."

"Why are you here?"

I'd been planning my speech but suddenly felt at a loss for words. I leaned forward, forearms on thighs, hands clasped. Silence stretched too long.

Lenore said, "Viviane, I don't have much time to

spare you. Why are you here?"

It was all so new to me, so surreal. There I was in a magickal land, talking with my great-grandmother who looked no older than my own mother, and trying to find the words to stop a war. Who was I kidding? I may as well have been playing with tin soldiers.

I took a deep breath. "I came because I want to stop all this. I want to make it right."

Lenore considered that before answering. "You can't," she said.

"So what? You're just going to go to war? Kill each other?"

"We have no choice." The sadness in her voice was ancient. "This war has been coming for a thousand years—ever since the Thu banished the Fomor to Gehenna."

"You do have choices," I told her. "You could withdraw your people. Live in my world. Maybe it's their turn?"

Lenore's eyes went dark and tight. "Never," she said with intensity. "Never will I give up Apfallon. We will die defending it, if we have to."

"Defending what? The land? How is that more important than people's lives?"

"You are naive. The people of Apfallon are linked to the land. Our roots are sunk deep here. Our cultures, our rituals, and our dead are entwined with Apfallon. Everything we are is tied to this isle." Lenore stood and paced, agitated. "It's our home."

I ran a hand through my hair, trying to find the right words.

She added, "What if an enemy invaded America? Would you just leave? Would your fellow Americans just pack up and go to Canada? Or would you fight?"

That struck a nerve because the answer that arose in my mind was immediate. I would fight.

"Okay," I said. "There's another option you maybe haven't considered."

Lenore looked on the verge of tears. "I've considered them all."

"Have you considered talking with them? Forming a truce? Sharing Apfallon with them."

Lenore threw up her hands. "Oh, Viviane. It's so much more complex than that. The Fomor are...bitter creatures. They would change Apfallon."

"Were they always bitter?"

She thought about it before conceding, "I don't suppose so."

"Hear me out," I said, "before you get angry. Okay?"

Lenore nodded, but her jaw was clenched.

I dove in head first. "Look, the way I understand it is that the Fomor believe Apfallon is rightfully theirs. Is there any truth in that?"

Averting her eyes first, then turning her back on me, Lenore said nothing.

I had to prompt her to continue. "Lenore?"

"It was once theirs, it's true. But that was a long time ago. We won that war, and Apfallon became ours—fair and square. They lost and couldn't accept it. Finally, the Tua sent them into Gehenna to avoid more wars."

"You exiled them from their home."

Lenore turned on me abruptly, eyes flaming. "No. We gave them a new home. And a purpose. They rule Gehenna. It's been like that for a long time now."

"What if," I suggested, "we could convince them to discuss a treaty? Approach them with compassion. Open a dialogue about how it would look if they returned to Apfallon to live alongside the Thu? Appeal to their higher nature."

Lenore stared at me. She huffed a small laugh and said, "You're crazy."

"Am I?" I stood and looked her in the eyes. "It's the twenty-first century, Lenore. We can lead the way into a new world. The old ways, the old wars, they don't work anymore. The Thu can evolve." I took a step toward her, hand outstretched. "What harm can it do to extend an olive branch and offer to talk before you pulverize each other and Apfallon? What harm?"

Lenore's lips parted, and she froze.

"Please," I said. "I can talk to the Fomor about it. I'm kind of like Switzerland."

"You'd have to go to Gehenna," she said, and I knew I'd at least hooked her.

I nodded. "No problem. I'm willing to do that."

"You're willing to make that sacrifice? Take that risk?"

"They won't hurt me," I said, though I wasn't sure about that—not after Rio's treachery.

"They might."

"Okay, they might. But it's a risk I'm willing to take."

Lenore dragged the back of her hand across her mouth and moved to sit back down. "Has anyone explained to you that—in order to get into Gehenna—you'll have to die?"

"Excuse me?"

"You're part human. You can't take your body into Gehenna."

"Oh."

❁❁❁

CHAPTER 9

Lenore was testing my resolve. Her gaze held mine, unrelenting.

"You're willing to die?" she asked.

My heartbeat accelerated. "What does that mean exactly? Die?"

Lenore sucked in a breath through her nose and sat back, crossing her legs. "It's not forever," she conceded. "Not unless something happens to your body."

"Soooo… I leave my body behind? Like when I'm jumping the moon?"

"Not exactly. Your body enters into a comatose state."

"Okaaaaay." I wasn't liking the sound of that.

"The transition into Gehenna will require that your corpus die. Your spirit will be released. Someone will have to resuscitate your body and keep it on life support while you're gone. You will, to all onlookers, be in a coma."

I stared at her, a queasiness building in my stomach.

She continued, "You'll need a plan and good allies. Someone to kill you and someone reliable to guard your physical form. Trust me. As soon as our enemies realize your body is vulnerable, they will go after it. You need to find a way to safeguard it."

I said, "Why do I have to die? Can't I just…" I didn't know what the alternatives might be, so I left that sentence hanging.

Lenore explained, "Gehenna is a unique realm. It has many names. Purgatory. Hades. The Underworld. Barzakh. Tamag. The Inferno. The Ur. It's the waiting room where the dead ponder and repent their lives prior to rebirth."

"So I've been told."

"Did they tell you it's terrifying, heart-breaking, and that you will not get out of there unscathed—assuming you get out at all."

I was making connections in my mind. My mother—Gisèle—had been a prisoner in Gehenna for most of my life. She was still there, held captive by my father.

Lenore and I sat in silence. I sipped my coffee, but it had gone cold.

How far was I willing to go? I didn't know these people. My family was Abram, Gisèle, and Colin. Was I sticking my nose in where it didn't belong? I could just walk away. I had no problem living in Reality. Apfallon wasn't *my* home.

And then, there was my mother. I said, "Gisèle is

there."

"Yes, I imagine she is."

"I know she is. She's been there all along. Trapped."

"Viviane, you're not thinking about trying to bring her out, are you? It's too late for that. She's been embalmed. Buried."

Tears stung the backs of my eyes and tickled my sinuses. I fought them back. "I just want to see her one last time. Apologize for not protecting her better."

Lenore sighed, and her sorrow showed on her face. "If anyone needs to apologize to your mother, it's me. You had no idea what was happening to her. Your grandmother and I kept her safe for as long as we could. Once your father got hold of her soul... Well, there wasn't anything else we could do but hope. And protect her body. We failed."

"Then help me. Protect my body while I go to Gehenna. We can make this right. If I can convince the Fomor to discuss a treaty, then Mom's death won't have been for nothing."

With a shake of her head, Lenore said, "I can't."

"What? Why not?"

"I can't compromise Apfallon that way. The Fomor could take advantage of you like they did before. They could send someone else—an assassin—back to inhabit your body, and we'd have no idea it wasn't you. I can't risk it. You'll have to find someone else to do that for you."

I said, "I at least need you to agree to come to the table."

She studied me, thinking, then replied, "If you convince them to do it, then I will as well."

"That's all I ask. Thank you."

She stood, folding her hands over her stomach with regal grace. "And now, I have duties to attend to. Apollo will see you back to your world."

Simon was waiting for me when I stepped out of the Poetry, Prose, and Poe bookstore—through the front door. As soon as I was out, I turned to thank Apollo, only to have the door slammed in my face. The lock clicked shut.

Simon's voice sounded in my head, "I see you made a friend."

I waved at the door and called, "Thanks!" Then rolled my eyes and headed up the street. Under my breath, I said, "Asshole."

Simon asked, "How did it go?"

"Fine," I told him. "Lenore has agreed to talk if the Fomor will also agree."

"That's done then. The easy part is over. Now, on to the hard part."

I pulled out my cellphone and dialed Corona. She picked up immediately.

"Viv!"

"I'm back. Can you come get me?"

"Totally. I'll be there in ten." She hung up before I could say anything else.

Leaning against the exterior wall of the bookstore, I rested my head back and closed my eyes. I was going to have to convince people who loved me to put me in a coma so I could travel to Gehenna, and I knew it wasn't going to be easy. Possible arguments buzzed in my mind, and I tried to rein them under control.

"Viviane," said Simon. "Pay attention."

A second later, another voice—one I didn't recognize—said, "There she is. I told you I saw her down here."

I opened my eyes to find a trio of young men stalking toward me with all the intensity of the Jets from West Side Story—but none of the music.

"Hey, Viviane Rose," called a second one.

"You might want to run," Simon suggested, and for a moment, I considered it.

"They'd catch me," I whispered.

Not one of the men could've been older than twenty, and they weren't Normals.

I pushed off the wall and waited for them to approach.

The first one, a Viking with white-blond hair and

ice-blue eyes, came to stand directly in front of me. I had to crane my neck to look up at him. He must have been almost seven feet tall. He still had something of a baby face, even squinched with anger as it was.

He said, "You're Viviane Rose, right?"

I put my hands up in surrender. "Yes. But look, I don't want any trouble."

"Oh, you done caused trouble a-plenty," said a burly young black man with a black beard much thicker than usual for a teen. He was wearing a letterman jacket with a stylized eagle on the left breast.

The third one was the smallest of the three, slim and only slightly taller than me. He put a smirk on his face and pushed the other two aside to get to me. I figured him for the leader. His golden eyes sparkled with amusement as he looked me over and said, "We heard about how you used to be in an insane asylum. Figures."

"Show no fear," whispered Simon right next to my ear.

"I've had a rough year," I replied, lifting my chin in defiance.

The bearded man said, "She don't look so special to me."

The leader laughed. "Guess you can't pick your rebirth body."

The Viking said, "I think she's hot."

"Listen, gentlemen," I said, trying to sidestep away from them. "My ride will be here any minute. I think—"

The Viking dropped a heavy hand onto my shoulder. "Where you going? We just want to talk. Get to know the newest wyrdo in town." I felt a chill pass from his hand, through my jacket, and into my shoulder—an unnatural coldness that made me shiver.

They all laughed, and I realized he'd done it on purpose.

"We should run her out of town," said the bearded man. "She broke the law."

I asked, "What law? I didn't break any law."

"She didn't break any laws," said the leader. "She broke the Fomor curse, though. And that's reason enough to throw her to the Kappas."

"Viviane," warned Simon. "You can't hurt these kids."

I felt three sets of hands descend on me, preparing to push and pull me. I raised my hands to defend myself. "Guys! Hold on now! You can't—"

One of them pulled out a few strands of my hair.

"OW!" I cried.

I heard someone clear their voice loudly, then say, "Locus. Gunner. Finn. Leave her be."

We froze in mid-action, and all four of our heads turned toward the voice.

A young woman stood there, hands tucked into the pockets of a down coat that made her look like a miniature puffball. A long, patchwork scarf of what looked like sari silk wrapped her neck and hung down in front and back. She had cherry red hair cut in bangs straight across her forehead where she'd painted on eyebrows in a shade of auburn. Her round face and doll-like lips radiated cuteness contradicted by the steel in her eyes.

I guessed her to be of Asian heritage, plus whatever magickal ancestors had contributed to her DNA. I could feel the aura of magick coming off her like a hum. I'd never felt that with anyone else before, and I took it as a warning to behave.

The young men did as well. They took their hands off me and stepped back.

The leader said, "Sorry, Mayor Violet. We were just—"

She cut him off, "I know what you were just doing, Finn McGee. And you should know better than to mess with a magick wielder you know nothing about."

"But, Mayor," said the bearded man. "It's Viviane Rose. The curse breaker."

Mayor Violet gave the man a direct, cold, and hard stare that was worth a thousand reprimands. She knew who I was. "Don't you guys have some work to do down by the river? I seem to remember you still have twenty hours to work off after that party you had down there. Don't make me tell your parents you left your posts."

The bearded man said, "But—"

Violet's voice dropped in both pitch and volume. She enunciated, punctuating each word, "Give her back her hair, then go."

The young men deflated.

The Viking held out his hand to me with three strands of my hair caught in his fingers. "Here," he said. "Sorry."

I took the hairs from him.

"C'mon," said the leader. He turned and headed back up the street.

The other two followed, and after a few steps, they broke into a trot. Not one of them looked at me again.

"I apologize for our rambunctious youth, Miss Rose," said Mayor Violet, stepping up to offer me her hand. "I'm Violet Bagley. Sorta the mayor here in Wyrdwood."

So it wasn't a jokey title. She really was the mayor. I was taken aback because she didn't look any older than the young men who'd just left.

I shook her hand. "Please, call me Viviane."

"Welcome to Wyrdwood, Viviane." She clasped her hands behind her back and looked away from me, perusing the line of shops on the other side of the street. "You want to be careful where you leave pieces of yourself. Others can hex you with them."

"Oh." I looked down at the hairs in my hand with surprise.

Violet changed topics. "I met with the city council this morning about fallout from the curse breaking."

"I'm so sorry that happened," I said quickly. "If I could've stopped it, I would've. In a heartbeat."

Violet smiled, and her freckles rearranged. "I'm sure that's true. But we have a situation now, as they say. It could get a lot uglier before it gets better. This feud between the Thu and the Fomor goes so far back and is more than skin-deep in both cultures." She sighed and paused to think before continuing. I saw her jaw tighten. "I'm taking steps to protect Wyrdwood, but you may want to leave for awhile." Her almond-shaped eyes lifted to mine. "For your own safety. I don't think those boys would have hurt you. They just wanted to scare you." She shifted her weight. "There are others, however. More vicious. Especially once the war starts. The kith of Wyrdwood can be...easily riled up."

"Mayor," I said.

She held up a hand, "Violet."

"Violet," I started again. "I have a plan to get both sides into peace talks. I already have Lenore's word that she'll sit down with the Fomor if they agree to it."

Violet tipped her head and studied me. "Is that so?"

I nodded. "I'm going to Gehenna to speak with the Fomor king and queen."

"King and queen? They're more like dictators, but okay. You realize how dangerous that is?"

"I've been told." I took a deep breath and sighed it out. "I figure all this is my fault. I have to fix it."

Violet chuckled. "You *are* crazy."

"No. I'm determined."

We stood in silence for a moment, then Violet said, "It just might work, depending on your powers of persuasion. Your best bet will be to get them both to a neutral location, and I s'pose that means here in Wyrdwood. If they meet here, we can control it, keep everyone safe, and keep it out of the Normal newspapers."

"That makes sense. Would you be willing to help with that, if they both agree?"

Violet chuckled without much humor. "Viviane, I'm afraid I have to insist on it. The alternatives are too freakin' risky. I'll start getting things ready, just in case."

"That means a lot."

"I wish you luck. If you can pull this off..."

Corona pulled up in one of the haven's cars and tapped the horn. I waved at her. "That's my ride. It was nice meeting you."

"I wish it had been under different circumstances."

"Yeah." I took a step toward the car.

"Viviane," Violet said.

I turned back to find she'd removed her patchwork scarf and was folding it.

"The night before you go to Gehenna, sleep with this under your pillow. Wear it when you go, hidden inside your clothes, against your skin. When you're ready to leave Gehenna, it will be your map—to Wyrdwood." She offered it to me. "You can give it back to me when you get home."

"Thank you," I said, taking it.

She nodded, then turned and walked back the way she'd come.

CHAPTER 10

I had to reach Colin. Once I was back at the haven, I locked myself in my room and tried to reach him with my mind and magick. Much to my relief, it happened quickly. I felt him. I sent a querying touch and was rewarded with his warm voice filling my mind.

Hello, love, he said. *Are you all right?*

I told him I was and what I planned to do.

Colin got upset. *You can't. It's not safe. You could die.*

"I might. I know. And it's okay. I have to do this, Colin."

No. My parents aren't interested in a treaty.

"We need to talk about this in person. Can you come here? To the haven?"

I felt his reticence, but he said, *I'll be there soon. I love you, Viv.*

"I love you too. I'll see you when you get here."

That was Colin on his way. I also needed Jake, Corona, Simon, and the "Lamby-kins" as Corona called the haven residents.

An hour later, we were all seated in the haven's common area with a warming fire in the fireplace. Ayu, as always, was quick to deliver drinks and snacks—in this case, lemonade and melted cheese sandwiches with bacon. They were exactly what the doctor ordered.

Colin sat beside me on one of the couches, but not for long. He was skittish and needed to pace.

"Jake," he said, "talk some sense into her."

"I've tried, Colin."

I said, "Please, everyone. Let's not waste time trying to talk me out of this. It's decided. Right now, what I need is to go over the details again. We all know that I go into a coma."

"More than that, Viv," Colin said. "Your heart stops. You'll be dead."

"Only temporarily." I stood and crossed to him. "If we do this smart, it won't be a thing."

Jake said, "I talked to Dr. Beaulieu earlier today, just to get some information. He's willing to oversee the process."

"Hey!" Corona said. "He's a coroner, right? If anyone can handle deadness, he can."

"He's a medical doctor first," Jake said with raised eyebrows. "I trust him."

Mr. Jorgenson asked, "Where are you thinking you'll store the body?"

"Here," Jake said. "In the haven, under the wards."

Booker raised a hand. "I can guide her in and the

come back to stand guard."

"We'll all hold vigil," added Hilda.

Carrie made a face and shook her head. "Ummmm, I'm not hanging out with a dead body." She wagged an index finger at us. "No offense, Viviane, but no way."

"Carrie." Jake frowned at her.

"No. No way. Uh uh."

I said, "You don't have to. No one *has* to do anything. It's a hundred-percent volunteer."

A cacophony of voices all spoke at the same time. Everyone but Carrie stated their intention to help.

Jake said, "Okay, okay. Relax. We've put a lot of thought into how this will work—and where it could go wrong. Beaulieu will help put Viviane into the moon. Booker, you will expedite her journey to the tunnel."

Colin said, "I'll meet her on the other side. She has to pass through the tunnel on her own."

Corona chirped, "Go into the light, Carol Ann!"

Several people chuckled. I raised my eyebrows and said, "You mean like... the light at the end of the tunnel?"

"Exactly that," replied Colin. "It's the transitional space between Reality and Gehenna. Everyone passes through it, but..."

"But?" I prompted him.

Colin said, "You'll be vulnerable there. I won't be able to protect you."

"Protect me? From what?"

"It's complicated, but from yourself? From the spirits who want your magick or who want to follow your silver cord back to your body."

I said, "Lenore mentioned that was a possibility."

Colin nodded. "If we're lucky, they won't know you're coming, so you won't have to deal with much of that."

Corona asked, "The silver cord? That's really a thing?"

Colin nodded. "The sutratma. It connects your soul to your body. If it's cut, you'll never find your way back."

Mr. Jorgenson said, "Or ever the silver cord be loosed—then shall the dust return to the earth as it was, and the spirit shall return unto the god who gave it. Ecclesiastes 12:6-7. I paraphrase."

"You're quoting the Bible?" I remarked, surprised.

"Of course. Truth exists in all mythic and religious texts."

I nodded.

Jake said, "Bottom line, we'll guard your body while you're gone. It'll be up to you to find your way back to it. Booker will watch for your return, and when you're back, Rio will perform the hex to get you back where you belong."

"Can we rely on Rio?" I asked.

Hilda answered, "It will be as easy as lying back down in yourself once you're here."

Booker said, "That and a little magick hoo-hoo.

We've got that part covered. Dr. Beaulieu knows the hex."

I asked, "So why don't people hex their peeps back all the time? It seems like a no-brainer."

Hilda cleared her throat. "Trouble is that you can't just come back. Once you're in Gehenna, you're locked in there—until Samhain."

"Samhain?" I tried to say it the same way she did, but it came off sounding like barnyard animals, *sow-hen.*

Jake answered, "Halloween. One night a year, the dead incarcerated in Gehenna can return to Reality to visit their homes, their loved ones, and their enemies. That is how you'll get back."

"It's an iffy venture, at best," commented Mr. Jorgenson.

The room fell silent, everyone lost in their own thoughts.

That night, Colin stayed with me. Making love was a slow, tender conjoining of our hearts, spiced with the fear of losing each other. Afterward, I lay in the dark, tucked against the curve of his body, and thought about the journey to come. I went over what I'd say to the Fomor in my head and wondered if Rio would be there. Would my mom?

Out of the darkness, Colin said softly, "Why don't you let me talk to them? I can maybe convince them."

"No," I whispered. "It has to be me, honey. I can speak for the Thu. I'm the bridge between the two races. If it was my fate to break the curse, then it can only be mine to fix the breach."

Colin brushed his nose through my hair, a touch of sarcasm in his tone when he said, "I suppose the worst that could happen is you die."

"If that happens, then I'll live in Gehenna for the rest of my time. You can visit me there whenever you like."

Colin's arms tightened around me. "I'd live there with you."

I basked in the warmth of his body and reveled in the feel of his breath moving in my hair. A worry rose from among all the others, and I asked, "What about your dad? Is he going to do something to you when you show up?"

"I don't think so," Colin replied. "That was all part of Nathan's and Rio's ruse. I doubt his lordship will even notice I'm there. I hope."

That eased some of my worry—a miniscule amount—and I was able to drift off to sleep. When I awoke, it was to find Colin wide awake on his pillow, watching me.

"Good morning," he said. "You were dreaming." His auburn curls were messy and wild, his presence naked and vulnerable.

I blinked the sleep from my eyes and smiled at him. "Probably about you."

"'All that we see or seem is but a dream within a dream.'"

"Edgar Allan Poe." I recognized the quote. It was one of Colin's favorites.

I studied his face. He was smiling, so precious to me. I said, "Tell me what our life will look like."

It was an old game we'd played at Malum, seated on a bench in the garden, watching the other patients stroll, mingle, and play Cornhole. We'd hold hands and imagine our life, taking turns describing it right down to the coffee we'd drink on Sunday morning.

Colin adjusted his head on the pillow and said, "We'll have a house in the country. White, with a barn and animals. Plenty of land, most of it forest. We'll have goats and a horse or three. Cats and dogs. You'll hang bird feeders all along the front porch so we wake up to birdsong every morning. We'll have kids. As many as you want. All magickal."

I blinked, surprised. Magick had never been part of our shared dream before.

Colin continued, "We'll have the fastest wifi in the county, and a fifty-inch TV in the family room where we can watch movies as a clan, sprawled on our sectional couch. With popcorn and hot chocolate. And we will never be apart again. Not like we have been."

I captured his face in both hands and planted a kiss on his lips. Rubbing my nose to his, I said, "I love you with all my heart." I couldn't remember ever feeling so happy. "You had me at horses."

After Colin left, I didn't want a heap of drama so I isolated myself in the room Jake had set up to house my body and waited for Dr. Beaulieu to arrive. Colin had gone ahead to Gehenna—to wait for me.

Jake had decided to put me in an empty room in Holly House. It looked almost like they'd cleared out a storage room for it. The only window was small and narrow, high on the wall. Outside, I could see the grass, ground, and trees, so I felt like I was in a basement. It was merely the underground side of the house, sunk into the hillside.

The aroma of bleach assaulted my nose. The room was cold and empty but for the hospital bed and equipment Jake had moved in the day before. I was glad I'd dressed warmly, including my red coat and the added layer of Violet's scarf next to my skin. I stuffed my hands into my sleeves and focused on practicing my speech.

Corona found me there.

"Hey," she said.

"Hey."

"You ready to go?"

"Yeah. The doctor's going to be here soon."

"He just rang the bell. I think Jake wants to talk to him first, before he comes up. He's pretty worried, you know?"

I nodded. "I get it."

"All of us are. Well, except Carrie. I don't think she has an emotional bone in her body."

I chuckled. "She's a funny lady."

"What's that?" Corona asked, indicating my pendant.

"It's an owl skull. A guy named Gore carved it. He gave it to me when I was in Apfallon. I think it's magickal."

"I'll say." She leaned forward to look at it, and I lifted my chin out of her way. "It's cool."

She wandered off, roaming around the room. After she'd made one circuit, she asked, "So, are you ready to go?"

"You already asked me that."

"Oh, yeah. I just want to make sure this goes smoothly, you know? I need it to go smoothly."

I took her in my arms and kissed the top of her head. "It will."

"You don't know that."

Distracting her seemed the best way to avoid her spiraling downward. I said, "You have to promise me not to go into the ocean while I'm gone, okay? No selkie hunting."

"I promise. My brother from another mother, Auto, has an e-mystery for us to solve anyway, so I'll be too busy to fret. He's awesome that way."

Corona had mentioned Auto once or twice, but I knew little to nothing about him. "Tell me more about him. His name is Otto?"

"Yeah. Though online he goes by Auto, like 'automatic.' It's kind of his schtick."

"How'd you meet him?"

Corona bobbed her head from side to side. "We were fosters together when we were little."

The door to the room opened, and Jake stuck his head in. "Everybody decent?" he asked with a dramatic tilt of the chin.

Corona called out, "Unfortunately!"

"Come on in," I said.

Jake entered, his smile tight but present. Behind him, Dr. Beaulieu entered carrying three bags and a plastic box with a handle. Not much taller than me, the good doctor had dark hair cut short, parted on the side, and slicked down with a product that made it shine like crude oil. His face was a bas-relief of hills and deep valleys, and they gave him a level of character seen most often in Basset hounds. Even his voice had the hollow depth of the breed's woof.

He sent a sweeping glance around the room. "Yes, yes. This will do," he said, walking up to the bed and placing his bag on it.

"Soooooo, what are you going to do to me?"

"You needn't wring your hands, my dear," Dr. Beaulieu replied. "I will simply stop your heart for a time. Once you have crossed over, I will restart it."

"Bud-dump-bump," Corona said, mimicking both a heartbeat and a punchline drumbeat.

I frowned at her. *My* heart was already beating overtime. "Just like that?"

Beaulieu nodded decisively. "Just like that."

"How will you know when I've...crossed over?"

The doctor cast a surprised look at Jake. "You do—"

"Yes, of course." Jake turned to me. "Booker will track your soul. It's one of his gifts. He will accompany you to the threshold then will come back to let us know you've gone in. Don't worry."

"I need a table," Beaulieu said. "For my equipment."

"We have one here," Jake replied and went to carry a card table over by the bed.

The door opened to reveal Booker backing in, pulling a machine with white tubes along with him.

"Ah, the ventilator. Very good," said Beaulieu. "Put it here, if you please. And bring me some chairs and another small table. Perhaps a cot. Someone will have to stay with her the whole time."

I stood there, watching the preparations, still wringing my hands. There seemed like an awful lot of medical equipment. Once he had everything set up to his liking, he turned to me. "Miss Rose, if you would please have a seat. I want to go over everything with you."

"Um, okay," I said. My nerves were jangling. I sat down with him.

The doctor said, "Please can someone get me a hot tea? I take it with honey."

Booker ran out with a muttered, "I'll do it."

Beaulieu turned his old-dog eyes on me and said, "You realize, I'm sure, that you cannot drag this out forever? Yes? The body—your body—will begin to weaken. Your muscles will degenerate, and you will be susceptible to infections. You only have a couple days until Samhain. Can you get what you need to get done in that time?"

"I think so?"

"You'll have to. If you don't make it back during this Day of the Dead, you'll have to wait a whole year before you can try again. Do what you have to do, then come right back. No dawdling."

"Okay."

Beaulieu took one of my hands in his. "You're sure this is what you want?" he asked.

I nodded, though I wasn't nearly as sure as I had been an hour earlier. "I have to."

"All right," Beaulieu released my hand and sat back. He took on a more professional demeanor. "Here is what we will do," he said. "I am going to give you a sedative that will put you to sleep."

"Like Mittens," Corona commented. Her nerves were getting the best of her.

Jake crossed to her and put his arm around her.

"Once you're asleep," Beaulieu continued, "I will insert a catheter and an arterial line in your arm. I'll also hook you up to an I.V. I'll monitor your breathing, your blood flow, and your chemistry. You don't need to know the specifics of all that, but suffice it to say that when you wake up—assuming we don't have plenty of warning—you may find yourself with many tubes on and in you. If all goes to plan, then I'll remove them before you awaken. I cannot promise this. Do you have any questions?"

I stared at him. This was all far more complicated than I'd imagined. Sleeping Beauty, I would not be. I thought, *Die young and leave a good-looking corpse,* and it struck me funny. I giggled, all jangled nerves and topsy-turvy emotions.

The others all eyeballed me like I had lost my mind.

"Will it hurt?" I asked, and my voice nearly abandoned me, so childlike and scared it was.

"Only when I put in the I.V." he replied. "After that, I will give you the sedative, and you will feel nothing of your physical form."

Booker returned with a mug, and Dr. Beaulieu

took it and held it in both hands as if warming them. "Make your peace. Say your good-byes. Let me know when you're ready to begin."

"No good-byes," I said, tears thick in my throat. "I'm ready."

Dr. Beaulieu nodded affirmation and stood. "Remove your clothes, please, and get into the bed."

"Wait," I said. "Will I be naked there?"

Corona gasped. Beaulieu shrugged and looked at Jake, who made a face. Booker had the answer, though. "You will be wearing whatever you imagine. Keep it in your mind as you go under. It will stick."

Booker put his hand on my shoulder and gave it a squeeze. "Remember to manifest a weapon. You may need one."

I gulped.

Booker scrunched his nose and nodded, then said, "Don't worry. You've got this."

"Thanks," I said.

"We'll step out until you're covered," Jake said, moving Corona toward the door.

"I have to go now, to prepare my spirit and mind for this journey," Booker said, taking up the rear and pulling the door shut behind him.

Alone, I stripped down, folding my clothes and placing them at the end of the bed. As I removed the scarf, I felt the strong urge not to let it go, so I lay it down on the mattress, then crawled in on top of it. I could feel its softness against my back and took comfort from it. I vowed to do something nice for Mayor Violet after I returned. I thought maybe she and I could even become friends.

"You can come back in," I called, carefully tucking the sheet and blanket up to my neck.

The others came back, minus Booker.

I focused on breathing—in through my nose and out through pursed lips—while Dr. Beaulieu put the finishing touches on his mechanical life support devices. He attached a clip to my finger, and my heartbeat became audible.

Pip.

Pip.

Pip.

The ceiling over the bed was painted white with a globe light fixture in the middle. It had texture and the occasional ding and dent.

Corona leaned in and kissed my cheek. She whispered to me, "Give my love to Gisèle."

"I will," I whispered back.

"And come back."

"I will."

Dr. Beaulieu pulled my arm from under the covers. Cool air closed over it like a caul. I held an image of myself in my mind, well-dressed in layers, warm coat, and comfy shoes.

Undies, pants, undershirt, shirt, coat, shoes, owl

skull, scarf. Undies, pants, shirt, coat, shoes, owl, scarf.

"A little prick," said Dr. Beaulieu.

I turned my face away and tensed even more. It hurt, but not for long.

Undies, pants, undershirt, shirt, coat, shoes, owl... scarf. Undies, pants, shirt...shirt...coat...shoes...owl... scarf. Undies, pants...shirt...coat...owl...shoes...shoes...

Pip.

Pip.

Pip.

"You're doing great, Miss Rose," the doctor said, his voice lost in a dream.

Pip.

Pip.

Tick.

Tock. The clock started.

CHAPTER 11

"Viviane."

Tick. Tock.

"Viviane?"

There I was. Lying on the bed. On my back. Eyes closed. Except I could see, and I wasn't on the bed, on my back. I was standing beside the bed. But not standing. I had no weight. No gravity. And I was outside myself.

A sudden feeling of falling made me reach out to hold onto something. All I found was Booker. He took my forearms and held me steady.

"Viviane?" Booker looked me in the eyes, anchoring me. "Take your time."

White noise muted the voices in the room, but I could still hear Dr. Beaulieu as he said, "Start the timer, Jake." He replaced the defibrillator paddles in their seats.

The heart monitor was screeching—flatlined. Something was wrong. I felt...wrong.

My mouth fell open, and I said, "I'm..."

Booker nodded. "Yes. Your body is. Temporarily. Remember? Once we get you to the tunnel, I'll give them the signal to start it back up. We need to go."

Tick tock.

I had a film over my eyes. Colors were muted, faces out of focus.

"Booker?"

"I'm here."

"I can't see very well."

"That's normal. Don't worry. I've got you."

I was dressed as I had been before getting in the bed, in comfortable yoga pants, a long-sleeved shirt over a tank top—layering because who knew what the weather would be like in Purgatory—and my red coat. I checked for Violet's scarf and the owl skull pendant. Both present and accounted for.

The moment my fingers touched the skull, the scum on my eyes broke free and slid down with a blink. I wiped it away.

"Gross."

"Ah, smart," Booker said. "You brought a charm. And you did great with the clothes. But where's your weapon?"

I immediately thought of the fireplace poker and felt the heavy iron as it appeared in my hand.

"Wow. Can I do that anywhere?"

"No. You have a few minutes to decide your appearance when you first leave your body. It sets like quick-dry concrete. You ready to go to the tunnel?"

"How do we get there?" I asked.

Booker quirked a half-smile and replied, "Have you ever wanted to fly?"

Before I knew what was happening, we were rising up, away from the floor. I latched onto Booker in fear, instinct kicking in. The last time I'd flown had left me traumatized.

He said, "Don't worry. It's safe. You can't fall." He moved close to my side and hooked his arm through mine. I hugged it tight against my body so he couldn't slip away.

My senses blurred as we floated up through what would have been the ceiling and roof then came back into sharp focus once we emerged outside. The trees dropped down all around us, an optical illusion that was persuasive.

In the distance, the ocean sparkled. The sky was Wedgewood blue, and pristine clouds swept across the sky. Wyrdwood nestled in the corner where the river met the sea. I felt sentimental about it, to my surprise.

"This," Booker said, "is where it gets surreal. Try not to panic. Just remember that I'm here with you."

The ground visibly rotated below us. I heard every detail, tasted all the colors, saw all the sounds. The cries of seagulls painted the air bright yellow. The green of the trees tasted like good scotch, and the clouds hummed as they melted into the spin.

"Is this what it's like...when you die?" I asked.

"It's different for everyone," Booker said. "For some peeps, it's like being washed down a drain or sucked into a tornado. For others, they're a Dervish spinning, or they're ballroom dancing. There's a lot of factors at play. Even when *you* die, like officially, it may not be this way. I'm smoothing your ride for you. It's pretty damn terrifying for most people."

"Well, thanks."

"Welcome."

We spun faster and faster until everything became a blur. Sights, sounds, and smells all merged into a great cacophony of light. I focused on the feel of Booker's arm tucked in mine, held tightly against my ribs.

Good luck, Viviane, Booker said in my mind.

His arm faded away, disappeared from my hold, and then everything stopped. Dead still. Darkness cut me off from everything. Booker was gone.

My feet pressed firmly into the ground. I was anchored by gravity again.

With careful steps, I put my hands out and searched for anything that broke the endless darkness. I put my hand out, feeling into the nothingness. The air smelled odd, chemical, the kind of smell that you taste in the back of your throat.

I was in complete emptiness, trying not to freak out. I stopped. "Okay," I said aloud, grateful for the sound of my own voice. "I can do this. All I need to do is..." I remembered the owl skull around my neck and touched my fingers to it.

A pinpoint of light became visible. I leaned left and right, just to make sure I wasn't hallucinating. It stayed in place. I couldn't tell how far away it was or if crossing the space to it would be safe. No other destination presented itself, however.

I inched forward.

The floor under my feet felt solid, and my footsteps echoed as if I were in a vast, empty room. The farther I went, the better I could see—either my eyes were adjusting or the ambient light was brightening.

A corridor emerged from the darkness. The moment I recognized it, I halted. Long and wide, it stretched for ages. Doors lined both walls. Twitchy fluorescent tube bulbs glowed on the ceiling. I was back in Vince Malum Residential Living Center—the even-more-hellish version.

Industrial linoleum lined the floor, chipped, cracked, and stained with various substances—the three Ps. Piss, poop, and puke. And blood. A rancid aroma hung heavy in the hallway—one of humanity gone sour.

Without premeditation, I thought, *Today, you're*

pain. Tomorrow, a stain.

The apple blossom wallpaper was gone, leaving only a chipped and peeling coat of paint—once white, now death gray. I remembered the pictures of flowers and landscapes that had graced those walls in the earthly Center, but in the afterlife, they didn't exist. The only de-cor—if you could call it that—was a long scratch someone had obviously made on purpose. It ran in spurts along the wall as far as I could see, reminding me of a keyed SUV.

I suddenly missed my friends from the ward. Eun Hee, Iraida, Calla, Dahlia. A wave of guilt washed over me. I hadn't contacted anyone since I'd left.

They probably don't even know you're okay, a mean little voice inside me said.

Lettie, my best friend since childhood, came to mind. I'd said good-bye to her, then had fallen out of touch.

You're a terrible friend, that mean little voice said.

I'd been busy. Between settling in at the haven, searching for Agate, rescuing Colin, getting stabbed by Rio, and breaking the curse—I just hadn't had time.

Bullshit.

I'd wanted to tell her everything, but I had no idea how Lettie would react to learning about magick, learn-ing that *I* wasn't all human. One day, I would. If I got out of the mess I was in.

You're a coward. It was my own voice, my inner critic come to life, harsh and bitter.

"Shut up!" I shouted. I walked forward into the hallway, and the hairs on the back of my neck rose to attention. On high alert, I made slow progress, afraid to step wrong, avoiding the cracks on the floor.

Step on a crack, break your mother's back.

I stayed as close to the middle of the hallway as I could and held on tight to the fireplace poker. Passing the first set of doors was nerve-wracking, but nothing happened. I paused and breathed a sigh of relief.

Too soon. Voices called to me from beyond the doors—unintelligible whispers and chants—nothing like the sweet, well-meaning voices of the residents at Malum. A door ahead opened a little with a creak. Darkness filled the crevice.

My body began to vibrate, my skin crawling. Instinct told me that to proceed was to die. My entire being recoiled at the idea, and I had to fight the urge to turn around and flee.

The light ahead—at the end of the corridor—beckoned me. Colin was there.

"Colin," I said aloud, just to hear his name.

Something moved in the darkness beyond the door that was ajar. Long, spikey whiskers—no, fingers like crabs' legs—stretched into view.

I heard a noise. Just over my shoulder. Reacting, I almost turned to see what had made it, but stopped myself in time. Nevertheless, at the edge of my peripheral vision, I caught the slightest movement of something retreating into the dark.

"Skisttterrrrri... Shhhhaaaaa... Maaaaaa... Pssssh-hh." The husky whispering escalated.

I made out words in the mix.

"It's her."

"Sweetness."

"She's here."

I broke into a run. Full tilt. Do not pass Go, do not collect two hundred dollars. I fixed my focus on the light at the end of the tunnel and booked it.

To say I was panicked would have been an exaggeration. I was determined.

As I passed them, doorknobs turned, and *things* came out. Only once did I glance into a widening threshold to find a roiling inky wall directly on the other side, from which craggy black fingers reached toward me. I didn't look again. They were malevolent, and that was all I needed to know.

The first of the spidery hands to touch me sent painful cold into my ankle. Carapace-covered fingers tried to catch hold and trip me.

Already my breath was coming quicker, and I

gasped, pushing into overdrive. I pumped my arms and kicked out to cover as much distance as I could, as fast as I could. I should have been getting nearer to the end of the corridor, but I was trapped in a nightmare. It remained distant, no matter how far I ran.

Another clawed fist closed in a handful of my hair. I wrapped my hand around the strands to keep them from being pulled out, and the tug tipped me backward. I nearly fell. I yanked myself free and swung the fireplace poker in an arc around my head.

I ran.

A stitch formed in my side, making it harder to breathe.

Time stretched to the breaking point.

Claws dragged across the back of my neck, scratching.

"Colin!" I cried, wanting—needing—help. I waved the poker more vehemently. My feet got tangled. A sudden wave of vertigo took the floor out from under me, and I fell to my hands and knees.

The whispers snuck in around me. "Pretty."

"Golden."

"She's ours."

I shouted, "Get away from me!" Scrambling, I got back up—barely. Exhaustion weakened my muscles and resolve. I took a few unsteady steps forward, then stopped. I needed to catch my breath. I needed to regain control of myself.

A hot wind from behind me brought the biting aroma of the sewer—so thick, it made me gag. I covered my nose and mouth.

The whispers had become a steady murmuration of mingled voices—raspy and chaotic.

Then, on either side of me, in the door cracks, the eyes opened. A dozen eyeballs emerged from the darkness on stalks, their whites reflecting the light ahead. Too round, they weren't human.

A scream rose into my throat and died there, choked by my fear.

Scrawny arms reached for me.

I menaced them with the poker, swinging desperately at any that got too close.

More hands reached... closer and closer... more than I could swat away.

Panic buzzed in my head.

"Get away!" I shouted, finally finding my voice. "Leave me alone!"

Frantic to escape, I lurched forward toward the light.

A wash of white hit me in the eyes. I stumbled again as a wave of vertigo challenged my balance, and my vision went crystalline, blinding me. Wildly, I swung the poker to keep the monsters at bay.

The poker connected with something far more solid

than the clutching fingers of darkness.

"Ow!" someone said. "Viv, it's me! Close your eyes."

Colin. It was Colin. His arms went around my shoulders to keep me from flailing any more.

"Stop before you knock me out," Colin said. "And keep your eyes closed."

I relaxed against him, smelling his mix of man and sage. "Fuck," I said quietly on an exhalation and dropped the poker to the floor.

Near my ear, Colin said, "You're okay. You made it."

"It was Malum, but worse," I told him.

Colin said, "Calm down now. You're safe. You're making it worse than it has to be. You can breathe normally. Remember, you're a spirit."

The light was still blindingly bright through my eyelids.

"Those creatures..." I was still breathing heavily.

"I'd have warned you," Colin said, holding me close against him, one hand pressing my face to his chest so my eyes were covered, "but it's different for everyone. I'm sorry."

"You mean it could've been a stroll in a garden?"

Colin chuckled. "For some, it is."

"The hell is wrong with me?" I asked, frustrated.

My beloved chuckled again. "You, my darling, are

a special snowflake."

"Shut up." I laughed, then asked, "Can I open my eyes?" I leaned into him, appreciating the warmth of his body and the strength of his arms around me. I'd made it.

"Not yet," he said. "There's something I need to explain to you first."

"Okay."

"You see..." His voice softened, and his words grew hesitant as if he were unsure. "The curse.... The Fomor curse...."

"I'm familiar with it." I cracked open my eyes to let the light in gradually.

"It keeps my people tied to Gehenna."

"I know."

"Some of us—those with mixed blood—can visit Reality, even live there, but when we're in Gehenna..."

The white light relaxed more, and my eyes grew used to it. I blinked several times.

"I know all that, silly," I said and lifted my face to him for a kiss.

Where I had expected to see my beloved Colin with his sparkling eyes, freckles, and auburn curls, I found a monster. The bone structure in Colin's face had bulked up, exaggerated and Neanderthal. His hair was longer, worked into thick red dreadlocks with black leather strips woven around them.

"It's me," he said, and his voice was Colin's.

My mind skidded, and my initial reaction was to pull away—violently.

He let me go, and I stumbled back.

"It's me," he repeated, then added quickly, as if trying to explain before I could run off. "Honey, it's me. This is my Gehenna visage. I was afraid to tell you."

"So you spring it on me like this?" I cried.

"I'm sorry."

I bent over, hands on knees, trying to get my emotions under control.

I peeked at him from under my lashes.

He had more bulk. I should have noticed it when he was holding me. He stood taller and his muscles were more pronounced. Everything was in proportion. There was just more of it.

He wore black leather pants and a billowy white shirt, untucked. The sleeves ended with a short flounce. The shirt lay open at the collar, showing a triangle of his sculpted chest. The old-fashioned romance of his attire contrasted with the bulkiness of his Gehenna body. Around his neck, he wore a thick, golden torque with turquoise balls entwined into the ends. The outfit was a far cry from the T-shirts and jeans he wore back home.

He held out his palms to me in surrender and let

me stare. "It's me."

"I can tell," I said. "You're..."

"Different," he supplied.

I nodded. My urge to flee receded. "Grandma," I said, "how'd you get so big?"

Colin laughed, a deep rumbling sound like his usual laugh, but larger, richer. He was himself, but more. "When you're done ogling me," he said, "we should get going. I don't want my father to have too much time to prepare before we show up. Word will spread quickly."

"I think," I said quietly, "I need you to kiss me."

Colin's eyebrows rose. "Is that so?"

I nodded and moved slowly toward him. "Just to be sure it's really you." I was afraid that if I didn't cross that distance right away, I'd never be able to do it while he was in his Gehenna form.

He let me step up close to him, and I slid my arms around his torso. I returned to the position we'd taken when I first arrived, my cheek against his chest, and I felt him wrap his arms around me.

"Hi," I said.

"Hi." He pressed his lips against my forehead in that gentle way he always did. I felt his love like a waterfall that gently washed over me.

"You smell the same," I said, closing my eyes. I lifted my face to him.

His lips touched mine, warm and soft, tender. He let me lead the way, and my entire being vibrated as I lifted up on tip-toe to make the kiss real. His lips felt fuller, harder, but how he moved them was exactly the same.

The tip of his tongue licked my bottom lip. I offered him the tip of mine in return, and the kiss deepened. He tasted like my Colin.

My body—not body—responded to him. My soul.

He felt so good. So solid and strong. His size made me feel small, and I liked that. I jumped up to wrap my legs around his waist, popping off one of my coat's buttons in the process. I didn't care.

He held me without difficulty. I wanted to be part of him, one with him. I'd never wanted him as much as I did in that moment. It was as if something primal in me was responding to the Gehenna aspect of him. I'd have gone all the way, right then and there. I'd have ridden him, let him take me, given everything I was to this man who was my betrothed, who was a prince of Purgatory, who would one day be the father of my children.

Colin, however, put on the brakes. He tucked his face into my neck and said, "Not now. Not here. Later, we'll have our time."

My arousal differed from what it was when I was in my body. It was an all-consuming fire that touched every part of me. Colin held me while my soul cooled. I lowered my feet back to the floor.

"Welcome to Gehenna," he said against the corner of my mouth. "My home."

No sooner had he said it than a flurry of running footfalls sounded all around us, and I looked up to find we were surrounded by people of varying sizes, colors, and genders. They all had exaggerated features, deep-set eyes, thick foreheads, and impressive cheekbones. The smell of a briny sea accompanied them. The tallest one looked ancient, his skin fish-belly white. He had auburn hair, darker than Colin's and stringy like seaweed. His face was gaunt and tight, eyes sharp. None of them could have ever basked in the sun or eaten a proper meal.

Their attire hung loose on their bodies, ragged but clean, and of varying shades of dark—tunics and loose pants—the weave visible in the cloth. Each one carried a long staff with a crook at the end, like shepherds—except the glint of the metal told me their hooks were razor sharp.

One of them stepped forward. His red-rimmed eyes had an unnatural golden tint that made them seem predatory. "Is this the Viviane Rose?" The way he said it made it sound like I was a new flower hybrid.

"Maaaaybe?" I replied, glancing up at Colin. I whispered, "Who are these people?"

Colin rested his cheek against my temple and whispered back, "Fomor guards. We should do what they say."

One of the guards bent to pick up my poker.

"We'll hold your weapon," the Fomor announced.

"Okay," I replied meekly.

The Fomor said, "You will come with us," then turned on his heel without waiting for a response. The crowd parted like the Red Sea to Moses, and we followed along behind him.

CHAPTER 12

A palace awaited us. We walked, surrounded by Fomor guards, through halls whose doorways were pointed cinquefoil arches. Elaborate mosaics covered the walls with tiles that evoked midnight and a full moon—indigo, white, and black. Detailed mandala patterns captured the eye and the imagination, presenting a far richer and more delicate decor that I would have expected given the hellish nature of Gehenna and the ragged demeanor of the Fomor. Still, evidence of the darker side of this underworld appeared in the cracks. One arching portico's mosaic included white eyes like those I'd seen in the tunnel. While obviously a decorative element, they nevertheless made my skin crawl.

I kept wanting to stop and stare, like a tourist, my neck craning to see everything, but the guards kept nudging me forward.

"What's going to happen?" I asked Colin under my breath.

He shook his head. "I'm not sure."

"Have you spoken with your dad?"

Meeting my eyes, Colin bit his lower lip and made a face.

I lifted my brows. "Does he know we're coming?"

His shrug said it all, but then he added, "Not much happens here that he doesn't know about."

The place was vast. I reached out to take Colin's hand as we headed down a ramped hallway with burning sconces to light the way. The smell of the gas had the unmistakable taint of sulphur.

We emerged into a cavernous room with giant stone columns carved to spiral upward. A crowd of Fomor waited there for us, watching us with unabashed curiosity as we entered.

At the room's perimeter, monstrous Fomor stood in clusters. The rustle of fabric and whispers moved through them when we came into view. Exaggerated body types—skinny, obese, hunched, long-limbed, short-limbed, and muscle-bound—gave the crowd a hodge-podge landscape. Their skin tones ranged from sickly white to inky black and everything in between. Overgrown and hairy, they all looked like they'd been living in the wilderness. They draped themselves in dark colors, their tunics and wraps of ragged material.

The citizens of Gehenna parted to make a path for us, and we headed toward the center of the room where a short dais held furniture that resembled the American White House's oval office—a heavy desk, a pair of couches facing one another with a coffee table between them, and a half-circle of chairs facing the desk.

At the edge of the dais, stood an array of fancy Fomor, those like Colin who had the means and wherewithal to dress in something other than rags. The only term I've ever found to accurately describe them is "Punk." I was overwhelmed by their overactive sense of style. I saw goths, steampunks, cyberpunks, werewolfpunks, deathpunks, and even a few glam-punks who stood out from the crowd—and that was saying something.

The colors of their clothes varied little. Blood red, midnight blue, obsidian black. A touch of metal—silver, copper, brass, and gold. Their hair was angry, molded into sharp spikes, shaved on one side, or braided into lines that resembled barbed wire. They ornamented their braids, dreadlocks, and mohawks with beads, bones, wood, silver, and gold.

Those Fomor, I would learn, were the magistrates—a council of elders who served and advised the king and queen. One of them dressed like a lumberjack, including plaid flannel, bushy beard, sideburns, harness, and axe strapped to his back. Another wore a tight-fitting cat-suit in black with a cloak of strung beads that rattled when he moved and would have made a nice curtain. A third sported a longcoat of black leather over a tight-fitted turtleneck and shorts that revealed tattoo-covered legs. She wore her hair in braids that snaked all over her head in intersecting layers.

We approached those three. I understood that whatever hierarchy the Fomor had, these three were at the top of that pile.

Colin released my hand and whispered to me, "Follow my lead."

I was all for that.

He stopped just in front of the three head magistrates. When he spoke, his voice carried and resonated with the power of royalty. "Has the Ardrí been alerted to my presence?"

Before he'd even finished the sentence, everyone in the room bowed their heads, and a shiver rippled through the lower ranks.

"Yes, Aubrey. I am aware." I was reminded then that they knew Colin as Aubrey, his pre-amnesia name. When we'd met at Malum Residential Living Center, he'd introduced himself as Colin. It was how I thought of him. I didn't see myself ever getting used to calling him by his birth name, Aubrey. The way I figured it, his parents chose Aubrey, but *he* chose Colin. Until he asked me to change, he'd always be Colin to me.

The crowd parted as the king, Colin's father, made his way to the dais. He was in his fifties or sixties, and he carried himself with authority. I immediately saw the family resemblance. His face was an older version of Colin's, but craggier with deep-set cheeks, strong bone structure, and a sharp jawline. Piercing eyes caught the light and consumed it. His hair was a mix of gray and ginger, messy like Colin's, but shoulder length with the ends twisted into tattered dreadlocks. Incongruously, he wore a knee-length pinstriped jacket, a double-breasted vest, and tailored pants that gave him an elegant corporate demeanor. His black shirt with its mandarin collar featured delicate white embroidery in an intricate design that sparkled with tiny white beads. A torque similar to Colin's, but with more gems, encircled his neck and rested against his collarbones.

He paused and stepped to one side, holding out his hand so that Rio could step forward and take it.

I instinctually took a step back. Colin's hand folded over mine, keeping me from going any farther.

Rio looked no different from how I knew her, although she was dressed up and then some. She'd piled her long black hair into a chic messy up-do, the white streak flowing in unpredictable curves throughout. Silver combs kept it in place.

Her dress flowed down her hourglass curves—scarlet lace, sleeveless, backless, and slit to her belly button. From her shoulders, a drape of translucent black silk spread into a train. Her every step was a mesmerizing tick-tock of feminine sexuality.

The mere sight of her put a bitter taste in my

mouth. My eyes narrowed, and I stared at her. Every bad thing that had happened to me was her fault. She had been the instrument of my misery for longer than I ever knew. The first time she'd wounded me—metaphorically speaking—was when she killed my mother. The second time had been literal. I would forever bear the scars from where she stabbed me—both physically and emotionally. If I'd been anyone else, I probably would have physically attacked her. The thought crossed my mind, but I'd lose in that cat fight. I'd get her back, one day.

Rio put her hand in the one the king offered, and they proceeded to the dais together. He guided her to sit on one of the couches and stood beside her.

"What is the purpose of your visit?" the king asked once the pomp and circumstance—and Rio—were settled.

Heads came up slowly, tentatively, as the crowd's curiosity got the better of them.

"Stop growling," Colin whispered to me.

I took my eyes off Rio and tried to put a neutral expression on my face.

Colin held out his hand. I took it, and he guided me onto the dais.

Everyone was watching us—all those strange beings, the Fomor, Colin's father. Nerves took over, and I opened my mouth to say something only to be stalled by a tight squeeze of my hand.

Colin turned to face me, turned me to face him, and took my left hand into both of his. He lowered to one knee with controlled grace.

I began to kneel as well, but stopped when he squeezed my hand again and added a swift shake of the head. I stood awkwardly.

He looked down at the floor.

I began to vibrate.

"Viviane Lenore Rose," Colin said, projecting his voice, "daughter of Gisèle Rose, daughter of Moira Gliton Rose, daughter of Lenore Gliton who traces her lineage to Aranrhod and thus to Tuatha Dôn herself, I am humbled before you as I request that you align your heart, your soul, and your descendants with mine. Viv, I love you with every spark of my being. I've wished on every star that you will still love me now that I'm fully revealed to you. Will you marry me?"

As he asked the last question, he raised his face, and his eyes met mine. I saw his love for me there, and I melted into it. We were already engaged, but that had never felt truly real. His amnesia and my hallucinations had always been a barrier between us. We'd known our plans could fall apart at any moment, if his previous life had suddenly appeared or if I'd gotten worse. And then, the car crash had happened, and I'd lost him—or so I'd thought at the time.

The earnest question in his eyes connected with my soul.

Magick coursed through me, igniting me with tingles.

Colin held up an antique ring cast in gold. It was ornate, with a lattice and ivy design. A large round sapphire held the place of honor, its depths dark, its surface shining.

I stared at it.

The room had gone silent—completely silent.

I touched Colin's face with my free hand, tracing the distorted Fomor curves that the curse had molded onto him. I felt the stubble on his jaw and ran my thumb over his lip. I met his gaze head on. Where normally my eyes would have filled with tears, they did not in Gehenna. That did not mean the emotions were any less powerful.

When I spoke, it rang out in the silence. I said simply, "Yes. I love you. Of course, I will marry you."

The room around me exploded in cheers.

Colin stood and pulled me into his arms. He kissed me, and this time, it held gratitude. We went back into a hug, and that was when I saw the dark look on his father's face. Rio, on the other hand, wore a smug smile.

Abruptly, Colin let me go and took my hand. He

turned us to face his father and said, "I claim this woman as family. No one shall harm her unless they want to answer to me. Father, this is Viviane. My future wife."

CHAPTER 13

An awkward silence hung in the wake of Colin's declaration. All eyes were on the king of Gehenna.

The man turned his head to meet Rio's gaze as he adjusted the sleeves of his shirt. Some silent communication passed between them, and I realized they probably were jumping the moon, speaking telepathically. When his attention swung back to me, something squirmed in my throat, and I swallowed hard against it.

With a voice that reached the far corners of the room, the king said, "Welcome to the family, Viviane. I back my son's claim of you and add my protection to his." No smile accompanied his words. The lines on his face indicated he may never smile.

A cheer went up in the room. Hands waved and shook in the air. Grins revealed the Fomor's teeth— crooked, black, sharp, and missing in many cases. I had the urge to put my hands over my ears—so abrupt and loud was the hullabaloo—but managed to refrain.

I almost missed the king's gesture that halted the cheering.

Without taking his attention off me, Colin's father

spoke to Rio. "Ríoghain, see to her orientation, please. I wish to speak with my son in private."

Rio still wore that smug smile. "It would be my pleasure, Husband." She stood and crossed the dais toward me, pausing only briefly to speak to a pale Fomor woman dressed in a black robe. She said, "Begin preparations for an engagement celebration."

The Fomor looked surprised and said, "But ma'am, it's almost Samhain."

"I'm aware," Rio replied dryly. "We'll celebrate tonight. There will be no interruption of the Hallows."

The Fomor nodded and bowed as she backed away from Rio.

Colin whispered near my ear, "You're safe now. Rio will take you to our rooms. I'll join you there once I'm done with my father."

"No," I whispered back. "Can't someone else? I could wait for you."

My hope died when he shook his head.

"You have to go with her," Colin said. "Just remember—she's the queen. Listen to what she tells you."

"But..." My energy had shifted, making me feel woozy and fragile.

He kissed me on the temple. "I won't be long. I promise."

The king had already turned away and was leaving the hall, expecting that Colin would follow him. Colin did, abandoning me with Rio.

I watched her approach with trepidation.

Rio stopped in front of me. "You're not going to faint, are you?"

"No," I said, and then thought, *But I might beat the shit out of you.*

A smile balanced out Rio's smirk. In my mind, I heard, *Follow me. We can go somewhere private where I can explain myself, grovel, and beg your forgiveness.* There was no contrition in her words, only sarcasm.

I hate you, I thought at her.

I know. Rio walked into the crowd, and it parted for her. For us. I followed in her wake like a handmaiden. She was in her own territory, and I knew I had a slim chance of getting any satisfaction from her. She'd have to walk a long, bloody mile before I'd forgive her for killing my mother or for almost killing me. She'd even killed her own son—right in front of me. I wondered if the king knew what she'd done. I realized I may have a means of revenge after all, and a spark of hope lit inside me.

Rio led me down twisting stone corridors with concave walls and irregularly shaped doors. A mosaic of black broken tile pieces caught and reflected the light from wall sconces. It was as if a Gaudí building had been turned inside out, and I was viewing it through a fish-eye lens. It did nothing to ease the upset tousling my spirit.

So, Rio thought, *this is Gehenna. You must have a thousand questions. I doubt Aubrey—I mean Colin—told you much about us.*

Is my mother here? I asked.

She is.

I want to see her.

I can arrange that.

When?

Rio stopped walking. *I'm not sure.*

Why not?

I don't know exactly where she is.

Well, find out. I need to see her. And you owe me.

The next biggest question I had sat like a knot in my throat, scratching to get out.

It's okay, Rio thought. *Ask. I won't lie to you.*

The question popped into my head. *Why did you kill my mother?*

Rio folded her hands over her stomach. *You have to understand, Viviane. I couldn't let anything get in the way of breaking the curse—no matter the cost. Sacrifices were necessary. Gisèle was just one midnight appearance away from telling you too much. All I did was sever her tie to Reality. She was never going to get better anyway.*

I gritted my teeth. *You don't know that.*

Yes, I do. Because I know why she's in Gehenna.

I took a step toward her, shaking my head. *Tell me.*

My dear, she thought without malice, *you don't want to menace me or even appear to threaten me. Not here or anywhere. I'm protected.*

Tell me, I repeated.

She is here with Chance. Rio sighed. *That's all I can say.*

Chance? The magic man from my mother's stories, the one who seduced her, with whom she fell in love. My father.

Rio continued, *I'll do what I can to get you a visit with her soon. She can tell you the rest.*

Soon, I insisted.

Rio nodded once then continued walking. Her tone returned to the tour guide cadence. She thought, *You should've seen the place when the Fomor first arrived here.* She ran her fingertips over a mural that stretched the length of a hallway. It depicted Hell as Western civilization had imagined it. Demons cast tortured souls into pits of lava and strung them up by various body parts.

Rio thought, *I'm sure you're familiar with Medieval paintings of Purgatory. Poor naked sinners abandoned by God. The Fomor's predecessors—Tanit and Baal—ruled Gehenna with brutal glee. One might call them sadists in today's world. The Fomor cleaned the place up and injected compassion into its rule. This mural serves as a reminder of what Gehenna was once like and what it could be again. I find it darkly beautiful, don't you?*

I had no desire to acknowledge that I did. I asked, *So now it's like a stay at the Hilton?*

Rio snorted a soft laugh. *Not quite. The whole point of Gehenna is to prepare you to reincarnate. You're given time to make your peace with who you were and what you did in your previous life.*

I snarked, *So, it's rehab?*

Rio wasn't bothered by my tone. She grew pensive and thought, *It's more tortuous than you can imagine. The blood-letting, the pricking, and the fire, however, are all self-imposed. The Fomor don't have to punish anyone. People punish themselves. Once your life is over, it's over. Amends are no longer possible.*

I asked, *Not even after you reincarnate?*

Most people, Rio said, *will never know they had a previous existence. They're not like you and me.*

She was sucking me into conversation with her. I asked, *Why give them a year if they won't even remember it?*

Because they will be judged at the end of their year.

Judged? By who?

The corridor opened into an interior courtyard surrounded by balconies and windows that looked down upon the cobblestone center. The ceiling was three stories above, and gothic arches rose to an ornate dome at the apex.

You're lucky, Rio thought to me. *You came at the perfect time. Samhain—what you call Halloween—is a time of celebration here in Gehenna. Every year at this time, the souls waiting for reincarnation are allowed to visit the living. The Fomor let them out, then herd them back when it's over. It's a sight to see, and one you'll never forget.*

I was unlikely to forget anything I'd seen in Gehenna.

Another question bubbled to the surface, however, and I asked, *Why did you send the assassin after Agate? What did she have to do with all this?*

With a frown, Rio looked over her shoulder at me. Aloud, she said, "The landvaettir? I had nothing to do with that or with the other kith deaths that Jake's investigating. Why would I? I have nothing to gain from that."

For some reason, I instantly believed her. Maybe it was the frankness with which she spoke or the almost offended tone. Maybe it was that fact that she'd owned up to killing my mom, or maybe it was because she spoke aloud for the first time since we'd been alone. Maybe I'd never really thought it was her. It never made much sense.

We stopped before a double set of walnut doors carved with half-human, half-animal creatures entwined together. When I looked closely enough, I saw many of the creatures were either having sex or murdering each other. Many were cannibalizing severed body parts.

Rio pushed open the door and stepped inside. She turned back to me. Aloud, she said, "These are Colin's quarters."

The room was a mix of midnight blue, evergreen, and red brick. It was all Colin—not the Colin I knew, but the Colin he would have been—if we'd made it out of Vince Malum Center. A warm fire crackled in the giant fireplace, and the furniture was made for comfort. A kitchen occupied the far end, and three other doors opened off the main room.

"Don't look so surprised," Rio said. "Despite what the Thu say, we're not barbarians."

"I know!" I said, sounding defensive even to myself. "I just expected something more..."

Rio finished for me, "Hellish?"

I shrugged. "Royal, maybe."

"Colin's not like that," Rio said.

"I know." Truth was that I found it comforting that Colin's tastes suited mine to a T.

At the far end of the main room, a bank of windows

offered a view of the jagged landscape of Gehenna from a thousand feet high.

The sky overhead was steely, and I doubted the sun ever shone there. No grass nor trees grew below. Where it was dry dirt, rocks of all sizes jutted up, creating a natural labyrinth of pathways that wormed from one dwelling to another. A main thoroughfare stretched into the distance, eventually swallowed by reddish-brown fog.

It, unlike the interior of Colin's apartment, *was hellish*.

Rio said, "I'll let you rest and change for dinner. You can't wear those clothes. I'll have something appropriate brought up."

"Thanks," I said before I could stop myself. Old habits died hard. I stepped deeper into the room, intending to ignore her.

"I've left something for you." Rio waved her hand toward a desk, then having had the last word, she turned on her heel, pulling the door shut behind her.

Curiosity won out.

A stack of notebooks sat upon the desk—my mother's journals.

A hunchbacked elderly Fomor with no teeth and a grizzled face showed up carrying a dress as gently in her arms as she might carry a baby. She lay it out on the couch, then asked in a scratchy voice, "May I help you dress, Miss Rose?"

No one had ever helped me dress except when I was off my head at the Center.

"No, thank you," I told her. "I'll be fine."

The woman withdrew a small make-up bag from her pocket and set it beside the dress. "For you," she said then headed for the door.

I turned my attention to the dress. It instantly captured my fancy. Rio was working hard to win my favor back, it seemed. The dress was high-necked enough that I wouldn't be embarrassed. Sleeveless, ankle-length, and midnight blue—one of Colin's favorite colors—it had glass beads sewn in a swirling pattern from shoulder to hem that made it feel great on—just enough weight to create drape.

It fit perfectly.

I stepped to the mirror and gasped, but not because of the dress—because of *me*. I'd changed. My magickal side had finally made itself seen. My ears had grown taller and more pointed. My hair was thicker and had a wavy life of its own. Most striking, however, was my face, the pointed chin, the high cheekbones, and the deep-set eyes. I stood there staring, mouth hanging open. It was me exaggerated.

No one had mentioned it. Not Colin. Not Rio. Surely they'd seen it.

I was beautiful, ethereal even, in a sharp-edged Fomor kind of way, and I had a moment of realization that it was all true. A hundred percent. I was magickal, the daughter of a Thu and a Fomor. As I stood there staring at myself, I felt the magick spark and flow through me. It was undeniable. Just as my engagement to Colin was now solid and real, so was my mystical ancestry. My bottom lip trembled with emotion.

How had I lived my whole life without magick? Looking back, the years seemed so dreary. In many ways, I'd been asleep the whole time.

I tore myself away from my musings and examined the bag. Inside was a pair of silk flats the same color as the dress, a comb, a hair tie, bobby pins, and a brand new lip gloss.

I used the comb and pins to tease my hair into a messy up-do and applied the gloss. Colin caught me still standing at the mirror, adjusting the pins in my hair. I almost didn't hear him come in.

"You look amazing," he said, setting my poker by the door. He'd rescued it from the guards.

I went to him and grabbed hold of his shirt with both hands. "Why didn't you tell me?"

"Tell you what?"

"About...this!" I waved my hand with manic circles over my face.

Colin didn't understand at first. I could see that, and then I saw when it hit him. "Honey," he said. "I thought you knew. This is how you've looked to me ever since you arrived in Wyrdwood. So beautiful."

"What?"

Colin blinked. "You're just now seeing your true self?"

I gestured broadly. "Yes!"

"Well, you're still coming into the Sight. Do you... like it?"

I met his gaze and grinned. "Yes."

"Me too." He picked me up in his arms and spun me around. When he put me down, his lips captured mine, and we kissed with feeling. It affected us both, shortening our breath, and urging us to cling.

Before long, we were both naked, and my up-do turned into a whole different kind of messy. The lovemaking was strong and intense. I felt things I'd never felt before. I had unending strength and energy, and my soul body could move in ways my flesh body couldn't.

When I came, it shot through me like a firework, exploding outward from my center, igniting me, and my whole spirit pulsed. He wasn't far behind, and as I felt him tense, I moved to deliver every possible ounce of pleasure to him.

Afterward, as we lay entangled together, he whispered into my hair, "We have a lifetime of this to look forward to." And my being pulsed again.

"I love you so much," I told him.

❋

We put off getting dressed to the last minute. He swatted me on the rump and said, "My father will be pissed if we're late."

"Can't we call in sick?" I asked, drawing a laugh from Colin.

"I'm afraid not. Fomor don't get sick. Besides, we're the guests of honor."

"Oh."

"Just think about how awesome it'll be to come back afterward, make love a few more times, lounge around together, and get up...together."

I swatted him on the rump in retaliation and said, "Yes! Get up! The sooner we go, the sooner we get back." I was already rolling out of bed.

One benefit of being a soul without a body was that I didn't sweat. Colin still had his fully-functioning body, however, and it turned out that I could get dirty—in all the right ways.

Sharing the shower slowed us down again—almost to the point of being late for our own engagement party. Afterward, we were sated, but we had to rush.

I kept hold of Colin's hand as we ran to the hall, and though we got there on time, we were both out of breath and flushed.

Getting into the great hall required that we descend to a lower level on a gazebo-shaped elevator. It was open on all four sides and offered a view of the vast room with all its many occupants. A half-circle of benches, set up in terraced rows like Greek theater seating, surrounded a stage. At the back of the stage, a row of high-backed, padded chairs awaited the royals. The king's chair was the tallest of all.

Fomor filled the benches, pressed in tightly next to one another, and they all stood when we appeared in the elevator. Their faces lifted to watch us descend.

A man with a great booming voice and an ancient accent announced, "Gracing our presence, Aubrey mac Bres and Viviane Rose."

I smiled and waved, which made Colin laugh.

"You don't have to wave," he said, then he waved too. The crowd broke out in grins and waved back at us. I was in love and high on happiness.

Like royalty, we walked together to the royal seats. Colin held my hand as I sat down in the one he indicated for me—the smallest of the four. Before I even had my bottom planted, he whispered, "Stand. They're here."

Again, the entire room looked up at the elevator, including me and Colin.

The booming voice announced, "Now entering, Ardrí Rebus mac Elathal and Ríoghain an Spyrys."

I leaned up to Colin and whispered, "I can't believe this is the new normal."

His laughter brushed my cheek. "After Malum, it's an improvement."

❀❀❀

CHAPTER 14

Colin's father and stepmother took their time crossing the vast room. They had both changed clothes and were decked out in matching all-white tuxedos. Both had ankle-length tails on their coats that flowed side to side in unnatural synchronization as they walked. Rio's suit had shorts instead of pants, but otherwise was exactly like her husband's. As they got closer, the pattern of veins on the fabric became visible. It resembled marble, except the veins shifted and rearranged themselves in a steady dance of light and shadow. It gave the impression that the fabric was caressing their bodies, which I visualized—then wished I hadn't.

Rio and Rebus smiled and shook hands like beloved politicians. I searched the crowd for my mother, but she was not there. No spirits attended the event—except me. I realized I hadn't actually seen any other spirits since arriving—only Fomor.

In a quiet corner, the Fomor started a chant that gradually spread through the room and increased in volume. "Apfallon! Apfallon! Apfallon!"

I remembered the point of my visit. The urgency with which it returned crashing into me like a tidal wave of ice water, dampening my happiness. A sudden onset of self-doubt made me hum with fear.

"You okay?" Colin asked, and I looked up to find him watching me.

"With everything that's been happening," I told him quietly, "I almost forgot why I'm here. I need to find the right time to convince your dad about the peace talks."

Colin nodded, his expression grave. "After the entertainment," he said. "He'll be more relaxed."

"Should I speak with him alone?" I asked.

After a moment's thought, he shook his head. "I wouldn't. If you do it in front of everyone, he's less likely to dismiss you outright."

The chanting continued, as it seemed to please Rebus. When they said it, the Fomor swallowed the "p" so that it came out sounding very much like "Avalon!" I made the connection with the mystical isle in the Arthurian legends. My knowledge of those old stories wasn't great and came mostly from television and movies. I made a mental note to do some research when I had a spare moment.

Finally, Rebus and Rio made it to us. Colin bowed his head as they approached, and I followed his lead. Rebus put his hand on Colin's shoulder and said, "Your duties begin tonight." Colin lifted his gaze to meet his father's eyes.

"I understand," he said.

Oh, how I wanted to ask, "What duties?" but I didn't dare. Not then.

Rebus moved on to me. I lifted my head slightly, rolling my eyes up to see his face. A crooked smile sat upon his lips.

"Viviane Rose," he said. "You are welcome here."

I smiled less crookedly than he, and said, "Thank you, Your Highness."

Rebus burst into a thunder roll of laughter. "I am High King, yes, but we do not use titles such as that."

"What can I call you then?" I asked.

"Most call me Ardrí Rebus or High Chief Rebus if you insist on speaking English."

"Forgive me if I butcher the pronunciation of your native language," I said, then added, "Ardrí Rebus." I did my best to say it properly.

"That will do," he replied, looking down his prominent nose at me. "I owe you a debt of gratitude for breaking the curse. I have heard what you risked to make that happen."

"I wasn't given a choice," I told him honestly.

"I know. But that alters little your importance to the outcome. Nor does it remove the risk to your life. Tell me..."

"Yes?"

He lowered his voice to a more intimate level. "You have not come here seeking revenge, have you?"

I blinked. "Revenge? No. Though I—"

"Good." Rebus cut me off. He promptly turned back to Rio and offered his hand to her. "We will speak more later," he said to me, though he wasn't looking at me.

Rio was whispering something into Colin's ear. She broke it off when her husband's attention fell back on her. Taking his hand, she accompanied him to their seats.

Colin and I sat as well.

With a wave, Rebus signaled the event to begin.

A Fomor woman stepped to the center of the room. She wore a gray sleeveless gown that draped loosely down her body and revealed the thick musculature of her arms and shoulders. Her entire head of hair was braided, looped back, and hanging down to her waist. She carried herself with elegance enhanced by the harsh lines of her face, thick eyebrows, and full lips. When she spoke, her voice was as clear as if she were standing right beside me.

"Tonight, we celebrate the union of our own Aubrey mac Bres with Viviane Rose. Viviane Rose brings the blood of humans, Tuatha dé Danaan, and Fomorian to the coupling. She, as you all know, is the hammer that shattered the Curse after so many centuries. We honor her for this, and we honor the union. Raise your voices in praise!"

The onlookers raised their arms and created an asynchronicity of cheers filled with slurring S, grinding CH, and cheering VAH sounds. Later, I would learn that they were saying, "Sláinte mhath," wishing us good health in their native language.

What then proceeded was a series of entertainers and raucous cheers for their performances. The first was a half-naked, thickly muscled pair of dancers, one man and one woman. Tribal drum music came from nowhere I could identify, taking the dancers on a journey of rhythm and punctuation. It took my breath away, not only because of their skill but also because of the beauty of their bodies, the tension and release in their muscles, and the way the oils on their dark skin made it shine. The dance wasn't erotic or romantic, but rather more of a celebratory expression of happiness.

The heady aroma of sage and patchouli worked its magic on me, and I began to relax. Food and drink were served to the Fomor, but not to me. I presumed this was because I was a spirit. I didn't get hungry or thirsty, so I wasn't bothered by it.

The second performer was a woman wearing a simple off-white shift that drifted around her as she walked to the center of the room. Her white hair was shaved on the sides, and the mohawk was braided back. Another woman accompanied her, dressed similarly. She was younger and had long black hair that hung to her waist. She carried a tray of foot-long skewers.

The performer bowed to Rebus and Rio, then to me and Colin. The crowd went dead silent as she then removed her tunic, pulling it up over her head to reveal her body, naked but for decorative chains wrapped around her waist and hips. Her large breasts hung heavily, the natural breasts of an older woman who has nursed children.

With flourished movements, pointed toes and stretches, she took one of the skewers from the tray, showing it to the crowd. All eyes were upon her as she inserted it through her earlobe and left it to dangle there. She did the same with the other.

Her dancing movements became more frenzied and strong until she stopped suddenly and firmly pushed one of the skewers straight through her breast, lifting it up to show the bloody end coming out the underside.

I sucked in an audible breath through my nose and latched onto Colin's hand. From then on, I could only watch in glimpses as the woman turned herself into a work of art, creating a symmetrical mandala of herself with the needles. I was horrified and enthralled. Even the blood rivulets added to the overall aesthetic of her performance. Droplets landed on the floor, and the soles of her feet were painted red by it. Her footprints on the floor gradually became a pattern made of spirals.

Fortunately for me, that was the most extreme act of the evening. I somehow survived it, though it remained indelible in my memories.

When she was done, the crowd went wild with their cheers. I released Colin's hand and realized mine was cramped from holding on so tightly. I joined the applause with much less enthusiasm. The performer received a standing ovation, and I rose to my feet to join them.

It was then that I felt the tell-tale twinge of pain in my lower belly and moisture gathering between my legs. At first, I was confused. I was only two weeks into my cycle. It couldn't have been my period. But then...something ran down my leg, all the way to my ankle. Surreptitiously, I lifted the hem to see.

A drop of blood was running down the inside of my leg. I checked the seat of my chair but saw no stain there.

With both hands, I grabbed Colin's arm and hissed, "I need to go to the bathroom. Now."

Colin studied me, confused. "No," he said.

I blinked. No? "Yes," I told him. "I think I started my period."

Colin shook his head. "Honey, you're in Gehenna. You don't have a body here. You're a spirit. You can't have your period."

I didn't understand. "But—"

A voice in my head said, "You're probably not going to die." It spoke with a Scottish accent and echoed slightly.

"Simon?" I said.

"Honey, what's happening? Are you okay? Simon's not here. He can't get to Gehenna."

"Here," said Colin. "Sit down." He guided me back down into my chair.

I resisted. "I'm telling you," I whispered harshly. "I'm bleeding." I lifted my hem to show him.

The blood was gone. Gone. It had been a hallucination.

"I..." Slowly, I sat down.

Colin lowered himself into his own chair but leaned across to me and took my hand.

To me, he said, "You're fine, right? That last artist was intense, I know. Just breath."

It wasn't the artist. I knew that. Nor was it real. The pain in my uterus was gone as quickly as it had arrived. There was no blood.

"I'm okay," I said and gave him a close-lipped smile. I was good at covering for my hallucinations. I'd had lots of practice. Thing was, I'd thought I'd left all that behind with Dr. Richard Reuter and the Center.

One performer after another came forward. They distracted me from my hallucination, and I began to enjoy myself again. Jugglers, knife throwers, fire dancers, and musicians took my mind off everything. I kept hold of Colin's hand whenever we weren't applauding, and he made no objection.

Eventually, the entertainment came to an end, and the Fomor woman with the looping braids returned to address the crowd.

"Tomorrow," she said once everyone had settled down, "begins the walk of souls—Samhain. For many spirits, this will be their last chance to see their loved ones. They will say their final good-byes. They will watch the living move on without them, and they will return freed from their ties to the past."

She turned in place, pointing her finger around the semi-circle of the crowd.

"Thus, it has always been and always will be!" she cried. "We stand beside souls in transition. We serve them as their guardians and their shepherds. We lead them—"

An anonymous voice called from the crowd, "Who will do this after we return to Apfallon?"

A moment of silence followed the question, and the speaker turned to face Rebus and Rio.

Rebus stood slowly. He folded his hands at his solar plexus and considered his answer before speaking. He let everyone's attention become riveted upon him before he said, "This duty—our duty to the souls in Gehenna—was not imposed upon us by the Curse. Our ancestors shouldered it when they saw how the souls suffered while waiting for judgment. They rebelled against Tanit and her consort, Baal. The Thu thought Tanit would enslave us, but we overthrew her and became the saviors of Gehenna."

Rebus took a deep breath, letting his sharp gaze travel over the crowd. He continued, "We are Fomorians!" He pronounced the ancient name for the Fomor with an accented lilt.

Whether we live in Apfallon or in Gehenna, we will always shepherd souls. It is our calling, handed down from our ancestors. No one else does it better!" With that, he raised his fist high, and the crowd cheered louder than any other time that evening.

My moment had arrived. I released Colin's hand and stood up. "Ardrí Rebus," I said.

The hall grew quiet again.

Rebus faced me. "Yes?"

I suddenly felt at a loss for words, but I knew I couldn't stop. I bought some time by saying, "I'm grateful for all of this and for your very generous welcome."

"Good," Rebus said and would have dismissed me had I not continued speaking.

"I have a message from my great-grandmother, Lenore Gliton." I put a bit more force in my voice to be heard over the rustling that had started as people thought the event was over. As soon as the last word was out, the room went dead still.

Rebus quirked an eyebrow. "Is that so? Please deliver this message."

"No one wants a war, Ardrí Rebus. Lenore invites you to sit down with her to discuss a treaty—one that will reunite the Thu with the Fomor, just like it always should have been."

Rebus's other eyebrow rose to join the first. "A treaty?" he said, and then his laughter rang out. Many in the crowd joined in. "That will not be necessary."

I gathered my courage and said, "You'd rather make war than create a peaceful union for your people? Apfallon can be your home. You and the Thu can share it. No one has to die!"

Still amused, Rebus tipped his head. "You're a child who has only just come into her Sight. We are a people twisted and hunched by millennia spent in a graveyard." He looked down his nose at me. "Why now? If the Tuatha dé Danann wanted peace, they could have come to us sooner. They *should* have welcomed us home. The only reason they're now suggesting this is because they're afraid. Now that the curse is broken. They. Fear. Us!"

The audience went wild. Fists and spit flew everywhere as they cheered their leader's words.

"Husband," said Rio. Her voice was soft, and yet it somehow cut through and quieted the crowd's noise. "You are right. They fear us, and that puts us in the superior position, especially for negotiations. We have the upper hand, and we can always fall back to violence if we must."

I blinked in shock when I realized Rio was supporting my plea, and she was doing it aloud, in front of everyone.

She continued, "Perhaps we should consider the Fomor lives that will be lost if we go straight to war? Our numbers have dwindled over time. How many would we lose?"

Rebus opened his mouth to reply, a hard look on his face, but Colin spoke instead, cutting him off. "A treaty makes sense, Father. And we have many demands we could make."

On a long inhalation, Rebus considered that, then said, "Where is my first son? I would hear what he has to say about this."

A voice rang through the room. "I'm here, Father." Nathan stepped out of the darkness in a balcony on the room's far wall, very much alive.

My breath hitched.

"I, for one, would love to see the faces of the Tuatha dé Danann as they realize their beloved Apfallon will never be the same—nevermore be theirs." Nathan shrugged in his nonchalant manner. "But that's me." Our eyes met for a moment, and I could have sworn he winked at me.

Rebus made a noise like a disgruntled bear. To me, he said, "They will come *here* if they wish to negotiate."

A sour taste spread through my mouth. I turned to Colin, "They'd have to die to come here, right?"

Colin nodded once.

I bowed my head in Rebus's direction. "Perhaps a more neutral location would be better? Wyrdwood. Mayor Bagley has already offered to set it up, and to keep both sides safe during the talks."

Rebus's hand curled into a tight fist.

I lifted my chin and added, "Please."

Gently, Rio put her hand on Rebus's arm. They looked at one another, and a silent communication passed between them.

With an abruptness that was startling, Rebus gave a curt nod and said, "Here are my terms. It happens on the final day of Samhain, and I will only do this if you, Viviane, mediate." He didn't wait for an answer but strode toward the elevator. Rio followed behind him, the submissive wife.

Nobody cheered, but everyone bowed, including me.

CHAPTER 15

"When is the last day of Samhain?" I asked Colin as we walked back to his suite. The thought of mediating didn't sit well with me. It was too much responsibility. If the talks fell apart, it'd be my fault. Of course, it was all my fault anyway. Maybe that's why Rebus made that demand—he knew I would do everything in my power to bring the talks to a positive conclusion.

"November 2nd," Colin replied.

"What?" I stopped walking. "Colin, that's in three days. Tomorrow's Halloween!"

Colin turned back and cupped my face in his hands. "Yes. My father has a strategy. He thinks he'll have the upper hand if he keeps everyone else off-balance. It's his trademark move. Unfortunately, there's nothing you can do about it. Once he's stated his terms, he doesn't change them."

"Three days? I have to get back to Wyrdwood. Warn Violet. Hell, warn Lenore." A wave of panic washed over me.

"You can't leave until after sunset on the second day of Samhain. November 1st. Until then, the veil will still be too thick for any but the most powerful spirits to pass through."

I didn't understand. "I thought Samhain was just Halloween."

"Not exactly," Colin said, taking hold of my hand to tug me into walking with him. "Samhain occurs over three days. The first day is Halloween. Starting at sunset on that day, Reality begins to shift into a darker spectrum of energies—a spectrum that will affect everything until Beltaine when it reverses direction. On Halloween in Western culture—although they've forgotten what it means—the living summon the dead from Gehenna with alcohol, music, sex, and the scent of sweets. They don't know it, but they're helping to pave the way from Gehenna.

"Over the course of those three days, the veil between Reality and Gehenna gradually thins, opens, and then gradually re-thickens. On the second day, souls can cross over. At dawn on the third day, the Fomor herd the souls back to Gehenna before the veil closes again and traps them in Reality."

"Why haven't I ever heard of this?"

"You probably have, but you—like many others—dismissed it. The Roman Church tried to take over Samhain—to rebrand it. They called it All Hallows and named November 1st 'All Saints Day' and November 2nd 'All Souls Day.' Throughout the centuries, the truth behind it has been watered down and commercialized. Few cultures still celebrate it as it should be."

"So, it's about honoring the dead?"

"It's much more than that. It's the time when souls can return to Reality and say good-bye because immediately after Samhain, they begin their transmigration."

"Transmigration?"

"Reincarnation."

"Oh."

"The living pay tribute to the dead during Samhain—each culture in its own way. Those tributes are felt by the dead and help them to find closure, say good-bye, and be ready to move on to their next life."

"If I can't go, can *you* go back instead?" I asked.

Colin nodded. "I can come and go as I please."

"Then you should warn them. Violet—the mayor—will need to know, and so will Lenore. You can get word to her through Violet, I think. If not, maybe Jake can help."

We had come to the last hallway.

"I'm not leaving you here alone," Colin said. "No way."

"I'll be fine," I said. "What could happen? I'm your future wife, remember? I have the royal seal imprinted on my backside."

Colin chuckled. "I want to see that." He reached for

my bottom, but I quick-stepped out of reach.

"I'll show you once we're in your rooms." I pointed at him. "But only if you promise you'll take the message to Violet."

"You drive a hard bargain." Colin slid an arm around my waist and drew me in tight against his side. Together, we entered his suite, and the sound of the door shutting firmly behind us was delicious. Seconds later, I was caught up in his embrace, returning his kisses.

I never actually fell asleep, though Colin did. I drifted into a meditative space where memories and dreams commingled. It was there that the sound entered my consciousness—at first, quiet. Gradually, it built to a screeching monotone that was horrifyingly familiar. It was the grind of death, the flatline alarm of a heart monitor, the shriek of a banshee that always accompanied a hag.

I sat up straight, eyes wide, searching all around. Colin lay on his side, faced away from me. I checked to make sure he was breathing. At first, I couldn't tell, but when he let out a soft snore, I nearly wept.

The alarm rang in my ears, a terrible tinnitus that I knew was only audible to me. I wanted to lie back down, cover my head and hide, but my instincts told me I wasn't any safer in the bed than I was out of it. Once upon a time, the hag had been in the bed with me.

I shook Colin, but he didn't respond. I shook him hard. Still nothing.

It was on me to stop whatever evil she was up to.

I got up and pulled on Colin's shirt and boxers. I slid my feet into my red sneakers without socks and picked up my fireplace poker from where Colin had left it. Then, I crept to the exit.

I heard, "Don't stick your nose where it doesn't belong." Simon's voice, deathly serious.

I whispered, "Simon? Are you here?" I received no answer. That didn't bode well. I wasn't sure what was real and what wasn't.

The hallway outside Colin's suite was empty. I stepped out, and the alarm grew louder. I didn't remember any other doors on that corridor, but there was one. The closer I got, the clearer it became that it was my destination.

Whenever I'd ignored Simon's advice, I'd lived to regret it. But Simon wasn't there. I knew it was impossible for him to be. The screech, the fear, and the danger were—I hoped—all in my mind.

I crept along the wall to the new door and touched the doorframe with my fingertips. My hand shook.

"Viviane," Simon said near my shoulder. "I'm serious. Stop. Please."

That time, I did. I stopped just outside, pressed against the wall. I'd been there before. I knew what waited inside.

The unearthly keening didn't waver.

I expected someone to say, "This is a test of the Emergency Broadcast System," but no one did. It just kept going. Other noises came from the room: grunts and groans, definitely human, and beneath it all, the resonant ticking of a clock. *Tick tock tick.*

I wrapped my hand around the doorknob, turned it, pushed the door open and rushed into the room with my poker held high.

The keening stopped. Everything stopped. I found myself in a large cavern with stalagmites and stalactites. Water streaming down the wall opposite the door and into steaming hot springs. I clutched my poker with all my might as a wave of vertigo overwhelmed me.

The centerpiece of the cave was a canopy bed with mosquito netting draped down on all sides. Other furniture occupied the space as well, and it was obviously set up for comfort. To one side, a fire burned in a large rough-hewn stone fireplace. The decor created a discordant ambiance of modern convenience and cave dwelling.

My system was on high alert, but I saw no hag

anywhere. What I did see was a woman seated at an old-fashioned make-up vanity with a round mirror. She wore an ankle-length peignoir in soft pink. It flowed down her body and pooled on the floor at her feet. With slow strokes, she brushed her long blond hair, the curls pulling straight then bouncing back.

Everything in me stopped.

"Mom?" The word came out all on its own.

The last thing I expected was for her to turn toward me, but she did. Her face broke with emotion, and she stood up on shaky legs. "Viviane?"

I crossed to her as quickly as I could, and she waited for me with open arms. Never in my life had I cried as hard as I did against her shoulder—my soul wracked with emotions I couldn't name. I hadn't experienced her holding me since childhood, and it felt familiar, natural—and more. It was the one thing for which I'd done everything. It was the reason I'd dropped out of college, taken the job at Malum, and stayed there for fifteen years. It was the reason I'd never given up hope. More than anything, *that* was why I cried. All my hard work and my sacrifices had led to that moment when I would hear her say again next to my ear, "Oh, my darling girl. I've missed you so much."

I don't know how long we stood there like that. Eventually my body stopped trembling. Though I didn't produce a single tear, my face felt red and swollen. I pulled back just far enough to see her face. "Mom."

She took my face in her hands, wiping my dry cheeks with her thumbs. "You're here," she said, eyes sad. "Does that mean—"

I cut her off. "Only temporarily. I have so much to tell you. There's so much happening."

A man's voice joined the conversation from behind me. "You'll have plenty of time to catch up. What a joyous reunion!"

I immediately recognized the voice but didn't believe my own ears.

"Chance," Mom said. "Please."

I looked over my shoulder.

Richard Reuter stood there. It was Richard, but not Richard. While I'd always thought him handsome, his attractiveness had been tempered by a lack of style. Before me was a man who knew exactly how to work his looks. He could have been Casanova or Rudolph Valentino, or George Clooney. He had it together. His hair had grown long enough to touch his collar and was full on his head. He'd shaved off the mustache and goatee. He wore all black—a simple blazer over straight-legged jeans and a crew-neck T-shirt. Pointed-toed dress shoes added to the polished-but-evil look.

I'd been thirteen when I first met Dr. Richard Reuter, the man who would be my psychiatrist for over fifteen years. I'd had sessions with him at least once a week, and sometimes once a day—especially during the time I was committed as a patient at Malum. He'd been my mother's doctor as well. The pieces of a very nasty puzzle were coming together in my mind.

"Richard?" I said, though I wasn't quite sure what I was asking with the question.

"Call me Chance," he replied with a cocky smile. "Or Dad, if you prefer."

"Are you kidding me?" A rush of anger or adrenaline—or both—flooded my system. "Are you fucking kidding me right now?"

Richard/Chance burst out laughing.

When I would have flown at him, my mom held me in place. "No," she said. "Don't."

My mother had written in her journals about a man who had seduced her and gotten her pregnant. She had gone into hiding to keep that child—me—away from him. My grandfather, Abram, had told me they'd used wards to keep him at bay. He had thought we were safe, but we'd always been caught in the spider's web.

"So," said Chance, rubbing his hands together as if about to start a task. "We don't have much time before your precious fiancé comes looking for you. I suggest we fast-forward the emotional reunion and get down to business. Vivi, I'm sure you have many questions, and we can have a session to discuss them all once Samhain is over."

My lip curled. "Session? No. You'll never be my doctor again."

"I suppose it is too late for that, given recent revelations. We'll have to work on what it looks like to have a father-daughter relationship. I'm looking forward to that."

I didn't know what to say. A barrage of thoughts ricocheted around in my head, and I didn't trust him.

Chance said, "You realize your mother can't leave here. I hope you've considered the idea of staying? Gehenna grows on you. If you live here, you can see me, Kypris—and I suppose Colin too—whenever you like." My mother's true name was Kypris. She'd used Gisèle to hide herself from Chance, unsuccessfully.

Chance continued with casual certainty, "We'll be a family like we should have been from the beginning. Return to Reality, and—well—you know what you have to go through to come back for a visit." He watched me and, when I didn't reply, he tapped an index finger in my direction. "Okay. You think about it. I'll check back in." His gaze switched over to my mother, and he blew her a kiss, "I'll see you later, my love." Then, he turned and strode out of the room.

The moment he was gone, I said, "I have to go back."

"Of course you do," my mom replied. She turned

me to face her again. "You have to go live your life, my darling. Life in Gehenna is no life at all."

"No, I mean, I *have* to go back to moderate treaty talks between the Fomor and the Thu. But Richard is right. Afterwards, I can live here with you. And Colin."

"Come," said my mother. "Sit." She guided me into the chair before the vanity and took up a position standing behind me. "Hand me the brush, please."

I did as she requested, watching her in the mirror. She was even more beautiful than I remembered, and I saw the family resemblance between us. She and I both had a fae quality, revealed by my strengthening Sight—a slant to our eyes, an angularity to our ears, and symmetry in our faces.

The familiar warm press of her stomach against my shoulder, the gentle stroking of my hair, the lavender scent of her—once again, I was overcome with emotion.

I said with a tremble to my lips, "He imprisoned you here, didn't he?"

"Yes, mostly," she said with acceptance. "I managed to leave a single thread behind, so I could see you and hear you. I'll never understand why he didn't destroy my body."

I said, "He wanted me. Finding you tied me to Malum. Your moments of lucidity kept me there."

"I'm sorry."

"Don't be. For many years, I believed you were dead. That's what Abram told me. But then I got the letter from your lawyers. I was eighteen when it showed up, and that's how I found you. Richard—I mean Chance—was already a big part of my life by then."

"My father? How is he?"

"Yeah, Grandpa's good. He came to visit me in Wyrdwood. I can't wait to tell him I saw you."

"And my mother?"

The question conjured up an image of Bella Rosenblum—a.k.a. Moira Gliton, my grandmother.

"Fine. She was never far from you, you know? I met her at Malum, though I didn't know then that she was my grandmother."

"I saw her in my dreams sometimes, whenever my connection to Reality touched one of her visits."

"She's the one who put you in Malum, right? To hide you?"

"Yes. After Chance took my soul, she put my body there to keep it safe."

"I see."

We both trailed off. I focused on the steady rhythm of the brush and relaxed a bit more. Such a vast web of deceit—nothing was what it had seemed.

"Do you like Wyrdwood?" my mother asked quietly.

"I think so. It's too soon to tell, and it's different

from anything I've ever known. All the kith. Apfallon. Oh, I met Lenore."

"You did? She's quite a force of nature."

"That's one way to put it."

A knock sounded on the door.

Mom called, "Enter."

Colin stuck his head in. "I got a message... Oh, Viv! There you are. I've been looking all over for you."

"I found her, Colin. I found Mom."

Colin came forward and held his hand out to my mother. She bypassed it and took him into a hug instead, saying, "No need for formalities. It's a pleasure to meet you. Thank you for taking care of Viviane."

"Actually," Colin said with an amused tone, "she's the one who takes care of me more often than not."

Mom indicated a circle of armchairs near the fireplace. "Will you sit with us for a while?"

"I'm afraid I can't," Colin said. "Viv, I should leave soon if I'm going to have time to warn Violet. The first day of Samhain has begun."

I got up and went to him. "Okay. What should I do?"

"Join the procession tomorrow, with all the other souls. Once you're back in Reality, you can make your way to the haven—to your body. Jake is ready with the hex to bring you back, and I'll be there by then, waiting for you." He brushed back the hair on my forehead.

"And Mom? Can she come too?"

"Sure," said Colin. "But...she won't be able to stay. Her body is..." To Kypris, he said, "I'm sorry."

"It is what it is," replied my Mom. "I'll try to accompany her, but it may be difficult."

"Difficult?" I asked. "Why?"

"Chance," she said. "He doesn't let me go back on Samhain. He says it will only increase my heartache, but that's just an excuse. The truth is that he's been afraid I'd be hexed back into my body. Maybe now that my body is gone, he won't object."

"What kind of hold does he have on you, Mom?" My heart ached.

"You, my love. He can hurt you."

"Not on my watch," Colin said.

"It's Richard, Colin." I told him. "Richard is Chance. He's had me and Mom under his thumb this whole time, and I never knew."

Colin couldn't have been more shocked. "Richard Reuter? He's Fomor?"

"Yes," answered my mother. "His magick hides him well in Reality."

"Motherfucker," Colin said under his breath. I could practically see the dominoes falling in his mind. "We're getting you out of here," he told me. "I'll come back and escort you myself. If I hurry—"

A feminine voice interrupted him from the doorway. "I will escort her." Rio stood there, dressed in a dark gray pantsuit with frills at the sleeves and neck. "You have one job, Colin. Alert Lenore. You may find that more difficult than you realize."

"You?" I challenged her. "I don't trust you to escort me."

"Well," said Rio, strolling casually into the room, "you could just stay here with your dear mother and father, and *maybe*—just maybe—Rebus won't care that you broke your word."

Colin's sigh told me how likely that was.

Rio continued, "If you want to ensure that she gets there, then I'm your best bet. I can get her to the front of the procession."

"She's not wrong, honey," Mom said.

My anger flared. "You don't know what she did, Mom! She killed you."

Under her breath, Rio retorted, "I had my reasons." More loudly, she said, "I'm trying to make all our sacrifices worth it. I'm not your enemy, Viviane. I'll prove it. What if I can get your mother back? Alive and well, in Wyrdwood with you?"

Everyone stared at her.

❋❋❋

CHAPTER 16

I realized my mouth was hanging open and shut it. Rio had begun pacing, waving a hand in circles at the wrist, obviously scheming.

Mom said, "I felt the last silver thread break. I have no body to go back to."

"True," replied Rio with slow deliberation. "But there are ancient means—Morrigan magick. More than one way to hex the moon." She stopped pacing and rubbed her chin. "Yes, it could work." She lifted her gaze to my mother. "Unless you *want* to stay here?"

Mom shook her head.

To me, Rio said, "I will escort you." To Colin, she said, "Get out. Go. Warn Lenore and the mayor. Hurry!" She physically pushed him toward the door, her tiny body versus his large one, and she won.

Over her shoulder, she said to Mom and me, "Be ready when the sunset horn blows. I'll meet you in Colin's apartment, not here." She paused on the threshold. "And, Viviane? Leave nothing of what you came with behind."

I nodded, and she left.

We had less than twenty-four hours before the procession was scheduled to begin, and I intended to spend every minute of it with my mother. I told her about myself and my life. She told me about hers, the time before and after she met Chance.

Eventually, we both ran out of steam.

She said, "You should try to sleep. Your body doesn't need it, but your mind isn't used to being awake for so long."

"I'm not tired," I told her, but it was a lie. I was losing track of what I was saying and forgetting common words. "Just for a little while, maybe. Can I lie down here?" Her big canopy bed was so inviting.

"Of course. I'll wake you in plenty of time to get ready." She pulled back the covers for me and tucked me in.

I don't know how long I slept, but I felt so much better afterward. My mind had returned to its usual pace, and I was ready to go. Mom dressed in navy slacks and a pink blouse, and we went together to Colin's Gehenna apartment. It was dark inside—and silent—until we stepped in. The lights came on, and an early Elton John ballad began to play. It made me smile.

"I love that man," I said.

Mom patted me on the shoulder. She went to the

wall of windows. "I hope Rio's right," she said. "Even if she is, though, we'll have to deal with Chance. He won't like me being out from under his control. We should probably go back into hiding."

"Yeah," I said, putting on the clothes I'd arrived in. "Because that worked so well for us the first time."

Mom laughed.

I said, "Don't worry. I have allies. They won't let anything happen to us."

"He might start World War III to have his way."

"He can try, but I'm never losing you again." I tied my shoe strings, then slid into my red coat. My iron poker felt cold to the touch when I moved it to the chair by the door. "I'm ready," I said. "Now we just wait for Rio to come."

We waited for what seemed like an eternity and watched Gehenna from above. From there, the people on the pathways were tiny, but I could tell which were Fomor and which were spirits. The spirits—like me and Mom—were smaller and moved in herds. The Fomor walked among them, isolated and on guard. They overshadowed the spirits.

When the horn blew, it made me jump out of my skin. The deep and resonant note reminded me of a ship's horn. I was sure it was far away, and yet the sound traveled.

"The procession is starting," Mom said.

Far below, a stream of spirits flowed toward the main thoroughfare and away from the palace. Various tributaries merged into one large river of souls—all going to visit their living loved ones. The Fomor stood out among them as dark spots that moved like hulking shadows.

"Shouldn't Rio have been here by now?" I asked, looking around for a clock. There were none in Gehenna, but I felt the familiar *tick-tock* of time slipping away.

Mom said, "We have time. I'm sure she just got delayed."

The front of the parade had reached the reddish-brown fog and was disappearing into it.

"Do we need her with us? Maybe we should just go."

"We need someone who can override Chance. He probably told the guards not to let us through. He's done that to me before."

"Mom," I asked, turning toward her. "Did he ever hurt you?"

"Hurt me? You mean physically?" She shook her head. "No. But it's been torture being away from you for so long. Chance likes to brag about how he can watch you, knowing it wounds me. His cruelty may be subtle and full of stealth, but that makes it no less hurtful."

We held hands, watching the procession stream into the fog.

"What if he did something to Rio?" I asked.

"He wouldn't dare."

Already, the parade was thinning out, and I suspected the end wasn't far away. "We need to go," I said. "She said we'd be at the front, but she's still not here." I strode to the door and opened it a crack. Mom came up behind me.

A ghastly Fomor stood in the hallway, his back to the wall beside the door. I shut the door again as quietly as I could.

Whispering, I said, "Chance left a guard. That's probably why Rio isn't here yet. She can't get past him."

"That makes no sense," Mom said. "She's the queen. No one disobeys her."

I pressed my palms into my temples, thinking, fighting the anxiety. "Maybe she put him there. What if she's betraying us?"

Our eyes met, and she was afraid too.

"We need to get to Reality," I said and ran from room to room, looking for another exit. There were none.

"They'll close the way once the entire procession is through," Mom said, sounding just as worried as I was.

"We're getting out of here," I said, reaching for my iron poker. I set it firmly in my grip and tested its weight.

"What are you going to do?"

I didn't answer. I put my hand on the door handle, looked back over my shoulder at where Mom was hugging herself, and took a deep breath. *Tick tock.*

I threw open the door and ran at the Fomor guard. He never saw it coming. I swung the poker at the side of his head and felt it hit. The Fomor went down like a deflated balloon.

Mom gasped.

I said, "Let's move." I wasted no time, struck out ahead, and hurried down the corridor. "How do we get outside?"

Mom came up close behind me, her fingers latching onto my coat at the back. "Up ahead—there's an elevator."

The elevator turned out to be magickal in function. It slid down the angled exterior wall like a slug on a slide. Mom latched onto a hand-hold, and I latched onto her. It took fewer than ten seconds to go all that distance, but still it managed to slow gently at the end. We stepped out onto a patio decorated with statuary.

All around us, carved in stone, were human beings twisted by pain and anguish. Cracks, breaks, and stains belied their age, and I presumed they'd been around since before the Fomor. Their eyes stared blindly into forever, like the ancient Greek statues that depicted gods and heroes. Their mouths warped with unheard cries and moans of torment.

I grabbed Mom's hand, and we ran through them without stopping and headed for the main thoroughfare. I was breathing harder than she was. As a matter of fact, she didn't seem bothered at all by the pace we were setting.

We were almost there when I felt a sharp tug on her hand, and it pulled from my grasp. I stumbled and looked back.

The Fomor I'd hit in the head had Mom around the waist. He was deformed, his facial bones asymmetrical and unnatural. With a heavy-footed walk, he headed back toward the palace—taking Mom with him.

Mom shouted, "Go, Viviane. Leave me."

"No!" I went back for her, poker raised high. I swung as soon as I was within reach. I hit the beast on the back of his shoulder. It barely phased him.

"Viviane!" Mom cried.

"I won't leave you!" I swung the poker again, jumping as I did so to reach the back of the Fomor's head.

He twisted his neck to glare back at me and growl, showing yellowed jagged teeth and gray gums.

"Let her go!" I commanded.

He did nothing of the sort. He half-set/half-dropped Mom to the ground and lurched toward me.

I scrambled back, barely keeping my feet untangled.

As big as he was, he had no trouble looming over me. His clawed hand scraped down at me, and I felt it dig into me—into my skin, into my soul. It hurt as if I were sunburned, and he'd scratched hard across it.

I howled, and my legs gave out. On the ground, I had no chance of hitting him in the face.

He reared back, ready to claw me again.

With both hands, I swung the poker as hard as I could, aiming for his knee. I struck first.

The Fomor's knee buckled to one side, bending at an unnatural angle. His attack missed me because he lost his balance.

I scooched to the side and swung again, this time aiming for the other knee.

He didn't have my agility. The knee gave out, and down he went with a loud grunt.

"Get up, Viviane," Mom shouted, offering me her hand. I took it and got to my feet.

We ran.

The Fomor rolled on the ground like a bug.

"This way!" Mom led me by my hand.

Not more than a dozen souls remained on the path to Reality, and that included us. We came even with the last stragglers in the procession and entered the fog.

❀❀❀

CHAPTER 17

"We have to get to the haven," I said, looking around. We'd arrived on a wide open plain covered with golden, knee-high grass. It reminded me of Illinois, it was so flat.

"Where are we?" Mom asked.

"No idea." I looked up to the stars, but it was overcast, and I couldn't see them. "Shit, shit, shit. I guess we just start walking." I headed off, but when was stopped when Mom didn't move. We were still holding hands.

Mom said, "There's a faster way. Remember. We're spirits. We're not bound by the laws of physics."

Booker had flown us. I'd floated over my body, and we'd zoomed through Gehenna. Old habits died hard, however.

Mom, already practiced at it, came up off her feet, tugging me upward like a child on the end of a kite. She said, "Just believe you can."

I imagined myself floating, and so it happened.

The landscape below spread before us, growing smaller the higher we went. The darkness didn't hinder my ability to see everything—and I silently thanked the little owl skull hanging around my neck—but I recognized nothing.

"We're not going to make it in time," I said, becoming upset. The higher we went, the warmer my chest grew.

Mom said, "Let's pick a direction and go until we spot something we recognize, hm?"

"Okay," I replied. "Which way?"

"You pick. Your instincts will be better than mine here in Reality."

"Where are all the other souls?" None of the directions felt right to me, so I just floated forward the way I was facing.

"I guess they get scattered around the world. We're probably close to a place that mattered in life to you or me."

A spark on the left side of my chest hurt—static electricity or an insect bite. I scratched at it.

Far below, a highway appeared. Headlights streamed along it. Still the plain was flat for as far as my eye could see.

"We should go higher," I said, turning my intention to doing so.

"I'm already having difficulty seeing the ground," Mom said.

"Don't worry. I can see."

We followed the highway, and the lights of towns turned to suburbs, then a city. I turned us toward it, and another sharp spark bit the left side of my chest.

"Ow!" I put my hand inside my shirt and rubbed the spot.

"Ow?"

"Something's biting me." I felt the scarf inside my shirt, lying flat against my skin there as Violet had instructed. "I think…"

"Are you okay?"

"Yes," I said, feeling hopeful for the first time since we'd arrived in Reality. I turned to our left. "It's the scarf."

"What scarf?"

"Magickal. The mayor of Wyrdwood gave it to me. She said it would guide me back home." The scarf sparked again on the left, and I course-corrected. A soft hum vibrated between my breasts. I was going to kiss Violet when I was myself again.

I gradually increased our speed, occasionally having to turn to keep us on the hum and off the sparks. The scarf made its will known. City after city passed below us, interspersed with wide swaths of land dotted with tiny lights—farms and homes. I spotted other spirits occasionally, traveling like shooting stars to visit the people, places, and treasures that were important to them in life.

We had to rise through the clouds as we crossed the Rockies, but the scarf kept us on course. As my confidence grew and as we got closer, I sped up even more until we were flying faster than the airplanes we saw. Mom clung to my hand with both of hers and kept up.

Eventually, Wyrdwood came into view below, the scarf radiated warmth, and I slowed to a more normal pace. I saw miles out to sea, where whales were breaching and playing. Cars traveled along Wyrdwood's roads, and homes glowed with warmth. Town residents strolled or jogged the streets, waving hello to one another.

We flew beyond the town center and up the ridge, away from the seashore. Animals in the forest below looked up as we went by—a white-tailed buck, a mama raccoon and five babies, and what was either a family of sasquatch or campers in fur coats. As the raven flies, it took us only another minute to get to the haven.

I descended, pulling Mom along with me. The moment my feet touched the ground, I heard Booker shout, "She's here! I feel her. She's here. Get ready."

We had landed in the open parking lot at the foot of the stairs. Golden light shone from the haven's windows, and I knew everyone was awake and waiting for us.

Rio flew out of Holly House and down the stairs, her feet just above the ground. "You made it!" she cried. "What happened? Why didn't you wait for me?"

I stared at her, my anger intense.

Mom said, "You never showed up! We were almost too late."

"What?" Rio said. "I went to Colin's rooms. We had plenty of time. They told me you'd already gone. I tried to find you in the procession, but I couldn't. I assumed you'd already come through." She sounded completely sincere, but I knew just how treacherous she could be. "You have to believe me."

"Not right now, I don't," I said. I scanned the windows, looking for Colin. Something moved in a second-floor window and drew my attention there.

Chance stared down at me, his expression as sharp as an arrowhead.

"Chance is here," I said without breaking his gaze. "Rio, are you working with him?"

"No. Absolutely not. He's probably the one responsible for the message I received."

"We don't have time for this," Mom said. "We have to get Viviane back into her body."

"Yes, exactly," Rio said. "This way." She turned to go back up the stairs, but I grabbed her forearm before she could get away.

"Wait," I said. "How are you going to bring Mom back?"

Mom came up beside me. "That doesn't matter, my darling. It's more important that your hex works. If Chance is here, he intends to sabotage your body. He wants you in Gehenna, and I have no doubt he'll go to any length to keep you there."

I said, "Not without you. Tell me, Rio. How?"

Rio glanced from me to my mother and back again. "With *my* body."

"What?" I stared at her.

"It's here. I can put Gisèle into it."

"In *your* body?"

"I figure I owe you that." Rio shrugged.

"You'd give up your own body?"

"I would," said Rio.

"Why?"

Rio leaned forward to look me square in the eyes. "To make right what I helped put wrong. My sacrifice brings the Thu and Fomor closer to peace. It's the culmination of everything I've been doing all these years. It's my role. My quest. My fate." She rolled her eyes up to the window where Chance had been. "We need to move. This way." She backtracked and took the path that skirted the forest. "If he catches us, this will all have been for naught." She levitated just above the ground, following the path up the hillside.

Mom squeezed my hand. "No, Viviane. You have to go first."

I tugged her forward, throwing my reply over my shoulder at her. "Either you go first, or neither of us do. I'm not leaving you behind." I gave her no room to object.

We followed Rio past Holly House and Cedar House to the back of the third building, Huckleberry House. Lost Lamb staff had their bedrooms there—everyone but Jake who had the fourth building, Pine House, all to himself. Rio waved a hand, and the front door drifted open. No one said anything as we moved through the house to a bedroom beyond the common room. A spark of magic unlocked the door, and it opened.

Rio's bedroom was not what I expected. Decorated with mid-century furniture in a black and white palette, it had a starkness that fit her only on reflection. Prints on the walls were evocative black-and-white portraits of people. Those I recognized included Abraham Lincoln, Mother Teresa, Albert Einstein, Martin Luther King Jr., and Robin Williams. The extreme close-ups revealed every wrinkle and quirk of feature, further enhanced by the contrasting light of the medium. They all had one thing in common—honesty of gaze and demeanor. I could have looked at them all day, and yet, it also felt as if I were the one on stage with all those remarkable faces watching me—as if I were among friends.

"Damn, Rio," I said, turning in place at the center of the room, impressed by the decor.

Rio shut the door, locked it, and sparked magick across the handle. Without responding to me, she turned and went to a large trunk at the end of the bed. More magick freed the lid.

Rio's body was tucked neatly into the trunk, in a fetal position, curled up as if sleeping.

"Are you ready?" Rio asked my mother.

Mom gazed down at the still body. "You're going to put me in there?"

"You do have the right to refuse."

"I really wish we were hexing Viviane first."

Rio said, "Chance is on his way. We have a matter of minutes before he finds us. Yes or no?"

I turned Mom to face me. "Yes. Do it, Mom. My body is safe. Jake and the others are guarding it. I'll be fine."

Rio was already weaving her fingers in the air, pulling strands of magical energy like silver yarn. One end of those strands was attached to the body, the other to her. She stretched them like taffy, whispering incomprehensible words of conjuring. "Hexing the moon," she'd called it. When you put a soul back into its body—or in this case, into someone else's.

"Say yes, Mom."

"All right. Yes. I want to live."

No sooner had she said it than Rio made a harsh gesture that ripped the cords from her spirit. She bent over in pain but didn't release the strands tangled in her fingers.

Someone pounded on the door.

With increasing volume, Rio's magical words—foreign to my ears—took on power. The pounding on the door escalated as well, as if they were in battle with one another. With a staccato shout, "Kiai!" Rio thrust her hand into Mom's solar plexus.

Afraid to interfere, I didn't move. I barely breathed.

The door to the room crashed inward. Chance's face was a mask of fury as he took in the scene.

"Stop!" he shouted, lurching forward toward Rio. He threw his fist into her face, knocking her back. Her hand came free, and she flew into and almost through the wall. She appeared to be stunned.

I put myself between Chance—Richard—and my mom. My hand wrapped a bit more tightly around my poker.

"Stop it, Richard," I said. "Just stop. This has gone on long enough."

Richard straightened and tipped his head, examining me, "Oh, Vivi. Family is eternal. You'll see once I get you and Kypris back to Gehenna. I've waited so long for all of us to be together. I won't let you run from me again."

"I hate you."

"No. You don't. You're just angry."

I heard Rio's body suck in a breath behind me.

"Yes, I'm angry," I shouted, sticking my index finger in Richard's face. "You've been lying to me my whole fucking life!"

He swatted my hand aside. "I did what was necessary to protect you."

"From what?" I asked, bitterness in my voice and expression. "You're the only one I need protection from. I never want to see you again."

"I know you," he said. "Better than you know yourself. I've lived every single day of your life with you. I've seen your every mood, failure, and triumph. I've seen you at your best and at your worst."

I unleashed the full power of my anger. "You stole my memories on false pretext. You weren't healing me. You were abusing me! Bullying me. You're not my father, and you never will be."

"Vivi, settle down. There's no one who loves you more genuinely or unconditionally than I do. Not your mother. Not Abram. And certainly not Colin."

Rio's body stirred in the trunk.

"Unconditionally?" I spat at him and stepped forward with every intention of pushing him back. "You kept my mother from me, locked her away, and threw away the key. You did the same to me at Malum. I'm starting to think you never would have let me out if I hadn't run away." I shoved a hand against his chest, but it went into him instead.

I was a spirit in Reality. The same rules of physics didn't apply as in Gehenna. I backpedaled.

He said, "I asked you to come live with me."

"Yeah, that wasn't creepy at all." I shook my head. "Just go, Richard. Get out." Desperation was making my voice come out sharp and squeaky.

Richard looked past me, and I dared a glance. Mom was gone, and Rio was unfolding herself from the trunk—except it wasn't Rio. Rio was still half in the wall on the other side of the room, both hands to her head.

Viviane, Rio thought at me. *You can't hurt him, but he's Fomor. He can hurt you! Run!*

"What have you done?" Richard screeched.

I thought, *I'm Fomor too.*

Richard's face twisted with fury. "This is not how it ends." He dug in his pocket and pulled out a gun. His eyes were on Mom, and I knew immediately what he intended to do.

Rio thought at me, *Run!*

In the next second, instinct took over. I held my intention firmly in my mind and raised the poker high over my head. It grew hot in my hand, but I ignored the pain and brought it down—hard—on his forearm. It made contact with a satisfying crack that sent the gun flying and bent him forward at the waist. I swung the poker back up, catching him square under the chin.

In my mind, I shouted at Mom, *Get out of here!* I had no idea whether she heard me or not.

Then, I growled at Richard, "You! Can't! Have her!"

"I already do," Richard replied.

I drew back to hit him again, and he plowed his shoulder into my throat. The impact knocked me back, off-kilter, and I slid into a dresser, feet barely touching the ground. He was off-balance and tripped along with me.

Nothing solid stopped my momentum, until I focused on anchoring myself in place. I passed through the dresser and halfway into the wall.

Richard crashed into me, shattering the dresser's mirror into a million pieces.

Seven years of bad luck.

The gun clattered to the floor.

I fought the wall's resistance. It wasn't as easy as I'd have wanted. I was still fighting my own concept of reality.

Richard shoved off the dresser and half-stumbled to where the weapon lay on the floor. Picking it up, he brought it around and aimed it at me. On reflex, I cringed away and heard the crack before I felt the bullet penetrate. It cut straight through me like I was nothing, immaterial. He couldn't kill me. I was already dead.

Like a banshee, I screeched with rage and stormed toward him, poker raised.

He fired again. And again.

I hit him. And again. And again. The poker burned into my palm as my magick heated it and made it solid.

Richard fell to the floor, curling into a ball.

I bent over and beat him for every lie, every abuse, and every betrayal. I almost didn't hear it when he said quietly, "Dawn." He reached for me with a bloody hand and would have gotten hold of my ankle if it weren't for Mom. She grabbed his wrist before he could touch me.

"Viviane!" she said. "Don't let him touch you." Though her voice had the timbre and depth of Rio's, I heard my mother there. "If a Fomor touches you at dawn on the last day, you'll be tethered to him. If you're still here, go! Return to your body! You're almost out of time."

I backed away from Richard, and sanity returned. Releasing Richard's wrist, Mom stumbled awkwardly toward the door.

Richard was crawling toward me.

"Take me to your body," Rio commanded. Weakened and shadow-eyed, she held out her hand to me.

"Okay," I said and grabbed her hand. I turned my intention toward flying after my mom.

A commotion behind me grabbed my attention, and I turned just in time to see Richard lurch to his feet and launch himself at me, a bloody hand in the lead.

"No," he shouted. "You're mine!"

I dodged to one side and blocked his hand with the poker. Momentum carried me all the way around, my intention strengthening as I spun.

He tripped past me, and I brought the poker down on the back of his head. The sound of the impact left no doubt that I had cracked his skull.

I didn't wait to see if it was enough. I focused my hate into the red-hot poker and hit him in the head again.

He landed face down and didn't move, didn't breathe, didn't blink. A pool of blood spread across the floor.

Spirit Rio, Mom Rio, and I stood over him, waiting.

"Well done, peaches," said a languid voice from the doorway. Nathan stood there. "Now that's entertainment."

I stared at him without a witty comeback.

My mom asked, "Who are you?"

Nathan ignored her.

Spirit Rio said, "You could've helped."

"Nah." Nathan leaned nonchalantly against the door frame. "Viviane had it under control. Besides, I'm just here to offer my darling mother an escort home." He pointed at Spirit Rio. "That darling mother. Not that one." He pointed at my mother.

My mother asked, "Rio is still here?" She couldn't see or hear spirits anymore.

Again, Nathan ignored her.

"I have one more thing to do," Spirit Rio told him.

"Ah yes, get our little princess back into her hot little bod." He looked at a non-existent watch on his wrist. "Better get on it. The dogs'll come sniffing if you're not tethered soon."

My mom looked at Nathan, "Viviane's still here too?"

"Yes, Mamacita," Nathan replied. "Your sweetling can't seem to take her eyes off the guy she just killed."

Mom's voice had an edge as she said, "Get her out of here."

Rio took hold of my arm and pulled me toward the door.

"They're going now," Nathan said. He offered Mom his arm, and she took it. They followed us through the haven, to where my body was waiting for me.

❁❁❁

CHAPTER 18

I awoke. Alive. The first face I saw was Rio's—Mom's new face. That would take some getting used to.

"Honey? Are you okay?"

I coughed when I tried to speak, and someone—Jake—held a cup of water to my mouth and lifted my head so I could drink.

"I'm okay," I said. "I want to sit up."

Booker stepped out of the shadows. "She'll be woozy for a bit, so stay close to her."

I had Jake on one side and Mom on the other.

I wiped the crust from my eyes.

Mr. Jorgenson stuck his head in. "Jake."

"Yeah."

"Reuter. Confirmed dead. We'll take care of the... mess."

"Thank you," Jake said with a little salute.

I breathed a heavy sigh.

Rio was there, a translucent form floating just above the floor. She smiled. "So, you can see me?"

"Apparently, I can," I replied.

"Can what?" asked Mom.

"See spirits. I see Rio there. She's—"

"Not for long," Nathan interjected. "Time to go home, mommy dearest. Dawn is breaking." He reached for her hand, ever so gently, and I saw the little boy he must have been—dark-haired, sullen, smart-assed, and quick as a whip.

Mom said, "It must be your Fomor blood. I can't see her."

"She's going back to Gehenna," I said. "Thank you, Rio."

"Don't thank me," she replied. "You owe me."

"I don't think so. You owed me."

She smiled first, and I couldn't help but do the same. I had, it seemed, forgiven her, and it felt good. I was so over having enemies.

The one person I didn't see there was Colin. When I asked where he was, Jake replied, "He stopped by to catch us up. He's helping Violet get the venue ready for the talks. They'll start tonight at sunset."

"We should go help," I said, wiggling toward the edge of the table.

"Oh, no," said Jake. "Not yet. You need to rest, to eat, and to figure out how you're going to mediate a cease-fire. You do not need to be setting up chairs."

The reality of what he said struck me. *Mediate.* Anxiety crept down my back to my belly.

My stomach growled loudly.

"Ayu has fixed you a feast," Jake said. "I think we could all use some sustenance right now."

"I don't know what I'd do without you all," I said, grateful beyond measure.

What are you supposed to feel when your father dies—and he was an abusive asshole? Richard was a huge part of my life for so long, and in retrospect, I realize that he *was* a father figure to me. I loved him, and I hated him.

He knew, from the very start, that I wasn't stalking the moon, and he preyed on my vulnerability. It could've gone so very differently. We could've had a loving, magickal father-daughter relationship. Instead, he chose to keep me in darkness and to reinforce my belief that I was mentally ill. It scarred me—in ways that will never heal. His crimes went far beyond what I'd thought they were.

So why was I so emotional about his death? Why were my feelings in such turmoil?

I was having one of those after-emergency breakdowns you hear about, sobbing silently into a pillow. Back in my body, the wetworks were unrelenting.

What is wrong with me? I wondered.

I sat by the fire in the living room at Holly House, alone with my thoughts. Mom was sleeping in an armchair nearby, and the others had all gone to assist Colin and Violet. Only Ayu remained, and she was in the kitchen—within shouting distance, if I needed her.

I'd murdered my own father. *Patricide. So cliché.* That was, I supposed, a factor in the sob-storm.

I fought the emotions. I pushed them down and wiped violently at my eyes. I wanted to feel triumphant. I'd saved Mom. Everything would be different now—better. And yet, I couldn't ditch a wrenching sense of loss. Truth was, I wouldn't miss Richard. I really didn't care that he was gone. I was relieved, and I refused to feel guilty about that.

My life would have been different if he'd never been in it—surrounded by love, success, and ease. Maybe Mom and I would have moved to Wyrdwood when I was young, and I'd have learned about magick the right way. I'd missed out on all that, and I felt *that* loss acutely. All those years I could never get back.

For so long, I'd been angry. I was past that, but in its wake came a heartbreak that I never knew was hiding just beneath the surface of my rage.

Watching Mom sleep—in Rio's body—felt wrong. She was my mother, but she wasn't. I supposed I'd get used to it. I hoped.

We'd already decided that she couldn't go to the talks. It would confuse both the Fomor and the Thu, and we wanted to give Rio plenty of time to explain it to her husband and her people. No one knew exactly how Rebus would react, but as far as we were concerned: *her body, her choice.*

CHAPTER 19

Corona came back to help me get ready for the talks. I put on a Pink CD while I dressed, because her songs always bolstered my courage. Corona must have been warned not to bombard me with questions. She was surprisingly docile, while extremely affectionate. We hugged on the couch for a long time before going upstairs to get ready.

"What am I going to wear?" I wondered. I didn't have anything fancy. Up to then, I'd had no reason to dress up.

Of course, Jake to the rescue. He'd thought of everything. Hanging in my closet were three simple, but elegant and finely made suits. The first was antique white, the second olive green, and the third was midnight blue—one of my favorite colors. All the same styles, they had wide-legged pants and a fitted jacket. Three cotton blouses accompanied them in the lightest shades of pink, white, and peach. It was the perfect mix of professional and comfortable.

I chose comfort for my shoes as well, slipping into my plain black sandals.

Corona painted my toenails for me, and that was lovely.

Make-up had never really been my thing, but I put on a bit of eyeshadow, mascara, and my favorite strawberry-flavored lip gloss. That was as far as I was willing to go, and besides, I wasn't the star of the show. Rebus and Lenore were.

I somehow managed to avoid being nervous until Corona and I pulled up in front of the Wyrdwood North High School. Violet had chosen the gymnasium as the best venue for the talks. While I was getting ready, Corona had described to me, in detail, how Violet had turned it into a wonderland, but I couldn't have imagined it until I walked in and saw it for myself.

The entrance to the gym was sheltered so people could drop off their families, then go park. The overhang was covered with blooming honeysuckle, and the aroma was intoxicating.

Mayor Violet had completely transformed the interior into an elegant ballroom that would have made Marie Antoinette jealous. It had chandeliers, a parquet floor in rich redwood, and flower arrangements on half-columns set around the room. A large round table occupied the center, surrounded by high-backed, upholstered chairs. More chairs lined the walls all around, presumably for spectators. Violet had obviously put a great deal of thought into everything. It took my breath away.

"Viviane!" called Violet, emerging from a side door

and half-running across the floor to me. She had a tablet in one hand and a stylus in the other.

"Violet, you've done an amazing job," I told her, moving more slowly than she to meet her part-way.

"Thanks, but it's almost time." She slid to a halt beside me. "Do you want to be here when they arrive, or do you want to make an entrance once they're all settled?"

I hadn't considered that. "I don't know. What's the etiquette?"

Violet froze. After a moment, she said, "I don't know. I don't think there is any."

"Okay, then I'll just be here waiting when they come in.

"Good," Violet said, tapping at her tablet. "You have a schedule, right? A plan?"

I didn't. "What kind of schedule?"

"You know. For potty breaks? Things like that?"

I chewed the inside of my lip and thought back to the laundry. *Tick tock.* "No problem," I said. "We'll take a ten-minute break every hour, unless things are heating up or going really well, in which case, we'll skip the break. Why don't you and I come up with a signal. You let me know when forty-five minutes have gone by, and I'll let you now if we should break or not."

"Got it. I'll send someone to refill your waterglass. That's the signal. You can announce the break if you want."

"Good." I said.

"We'll have security all around, outside the gym as well," Violet said. "If you need help, or a fast exit, make for that security door." She pointed out the double emergency exit. "It goes straight to the patio and into the arms of several magickal guards. They'll get you to safety."

"Wow," I said. "You've thought of everything."

Violet patted me on the arm. "Please, gods, I hope so."

I stood at the far end of the table, facing the doorway, as the Fomor entered. First came six scouts who spread out, checking security before letting Rebus come through. They searched thoroughly under every chair, crawled under the table, and noted every detail, calling out to one another about exits, line of sight, and possible locations for surveillance devices. They were done in ten minutes and alerted Rebus with a brisk, "All clear!" They then took up positions around the perimeter.

Rebus was escorted in. In Reality, his features lost the cragginess that they'd had in Gehenna, and he could have been a fashion model. His hair was his most striking feature. Still ginger mixed with silver, the dreadlocks were gone. It flowed straight back from his forehead in thick waves.

He wore a double-breasted and fitted banyan of midnight blue. It covered him to mid-calf and was embroidered with silver thread in a marble pattern. Underneath, showing from the hem to the ankles of his Roman sandals, was a silver skirt in pleated tulle. On his head, he wore a braided silver crown with a three-inch dark marquise-cut sapphire that could have been the doorway to another dimension. He was impressive, to say the least.

Rio was, of course, not attending. As far as I knew, a spirit couldn't leave Gehenna except on the second night of Samhain. It hit me suddenly just what a sacrifice she had made for me and Mom. I stood a little taller, thinking maybe I did owe her.

Nathan and—more importantly—Colin followed Rebus in, both dressed to the nines in what must have been the Fomor ceremonial garb. Black velvet bolero jackets with high collars, silver buttons, épaulettes, and straight-leg pants.

Colin's face had returned to what I knew best. I decided the softer look suited him—and me—better. My love for him asserted itself, swelling in my heart.

At the sight of me, Colin burst into a grin. I returned it with a bright one of my own.

Lenore came next with her guards in diamond formation around her. A troll led the procession, his hulking figure a warning not to mess with his mistress. Lenore rode on the back of the centaur from Bella's scrying. The centaur wore ceremonial armor hammered to fit exactly to her body, including breasts and full figure. A second piece covered her back and hindquarters. A finely decorated leather saddle was strapped atop the armor.

Lenore wore a cream-colored, satin corset with wide shoulder straps—simple in design, but elegant—and doe-skin breeches decorated with burned-in swirls in a labyrinthine pattern. Her thigh-high boots—the same shade as the burns—complemented them.

Over the top, a translucent duster of light blue rippled loosely around her, alive with subtle movement. Clouds streamed across its surface, creating the illusion of a summer sky. The overcoat's train and sleeves ran loosely down to her knees and wrists.

Her silver hair was teased up into a bouffant style with small, glittering diamonds all over. She was my great-grandmother, and I was humbled by her regal beauty.

A man dressed all in red brought forth a box when the centaur stopped. He shook it once, then set it on the floor. A set of stairs toppled up and out. The man offered Lenore his hand, and she descended with grace.

I watched as her attendant helped her to her seat and realized she was working hard to cover her physical frailty—maybe even using magick to hide it. She couldn't hide it all though. I saw through her glamour.

Rebus had chosen his side of the table, and Lenore took her place opposite. They nodded to one another, then sat simultaneously. I figured we were off to a good start.

I remained on my feet and waited until everyone was settled. Then, I said, "I want to thank you both for giving this a chance. I'm excited about the possibilities of what we can accomplish here, and—"

Rebus interrupted me, "Future daughter-in-law," he said, "can we get down to business? The longer I'm here, the more irritated I become."

I blinked and realized I was outmatched. In two sentences, he had put me in my place, announced to the room that he had a special relationship with me, and re-minded me that I had an obligation to the Fomor—or so he thought.

"Yes," I said. "Of course. I believe you've both brought your list of demands with you, am I right?"

Lenore was looking anywhere but at Rebus. "That's correct," she said.

Rebus nodded and waved a hand to one of his at-tendants who produced a roll of paper from inside his coat. He spread it upon the table—and continued spread-ing it. It was nearly a yard long.

I sighed. "Okay. Why don't we do this? Ardrí Rebus, what is your number one demand? The one thing that, if not granted, will be a deal-breaker?"

"One?" mocked Rebus.

"For now. The most important one."

Rebus chewed his tongue, then said, "The Fomor will be restored as the rightful rulers of Apfallon."

Lenore made a face and actually rolled her eyes.

I swallowed. "Well, that's a starting point for negotiations. Now, Lady Lenore. What is your number one?"

Without hesitation, Lenore said, "The Fomor will withdraw their army from the shores of Apfallon and threaten us no longer."

The people in the spectator seats began to whisper to one another.

"Shut up!" Violet shouted, and the room went silent. "Anyone who does not respect the rules will be ousted with prejudice. No noise from the peanut gallery."

Shaken, I hesitated. Rebus and Lenore were both watching me, waiting to see what my next move was.

I shook myself and said, "That's a great start. As I understand it, Apfallon is currently ruled by a council of counties. What if we reimagined that? Is there a section of Apfallon that could be Fomor County, for example? With Ardrí Rebus a full-fledged representative on the ruling council."

"What do I look like?" Rebus bellowed. "I'm no lord! I'm a king. High king."

"You're king in your own mind," said Lenore just loud enough to be heard. She rolled her eyes again.

Rebus stood. "And now she insults me. This is over."

Not five minutes into it, I was losing control. I sensed a crash coming, and panic forced me to act without thinking first.

"Ardrí Rebus!" I said, vehement. "You cannot leave. You owe it to your people to try to make this work." I turned on Lenore. "And you, Great-grandmother, owe it to yours. You both come from great families—families that have intermingled throughout the millennia to bring us to this time and place. We are all related. One family. I am Fomor as much as I am Tuatha dé Danann as much as I am human. And I'm not alone. Many in this room come from mixed ancestry. To pretend you're better or worse than anyone else is ridiculous in this day and age."

Slowly, Rebus resumed his seat.

Lenore watched me, gaze direct and unchallenging. She even nodded slightly.

I continued in a somewhat less aggressive tone. "The reality is that the world has evolved. It's time for us—the kith—to evolve too. This feud goes back to a time no one remembers. It's foolish at best and self-destructive at worst. Apfallon is beautiful, and I understand why the Fomor want to return there. The emerald hills, open skies, and land alive with magick. I get it.

"Gehenna is also beautiful and serves a purpose that Apfallon benefits from. Its history goes back, perhaps even farther than Apfallon's, to a time when old gods ruled with ham-fisted cruelty. The city is a work of art—a testimonial to the improvements the Fomor have made there. It's a *safe* haven for souls in transit, and while its magick comes from a deeper, darker source, it is no less powerful.

"I know there is a middle-ground here. We don't have to cling to the ignorant grudges of primitive ancestors. Let's do better. For everyone. You've got an opportunity here, both of you, to set an example for the rest of the kith, for future generations."

"Can't we all just get along?" said a snide voice. Nathan.

I glared at him. "I know it's not that simple, but we're smarter and more sophisticated than our ancestors. We don't live in the same world they did." I forced my shoulders to relax, then added, "The Fomor have earned their right to share Apfallon by taking care of our dead for so many generations. I've seen with my own eyes how the Fomor handle souls with respect and compassion."

Nathan's eyebrows raised. His mouth went slack,

and the sass left his expression.

Lenore took a slow, deep breath.

I said, "No one has challenged the curse—until now. The time has come to make amends and to fix what was broken. How about we roll up our sleeves and get started, okay? 'Cause this treaty isn't going to write itself. It's time to step into the twenty-first century. The future is in our hands—right here, right now."

Finally, I sat down—mostly because my legs were shaking.

Lenore nodded.

Rebus grunted.

And thus, the talks got underway.

CHAPTER 20

Three long days of talking, arguing, and negotiating passed without anyone dying or maimed, much to my surprise. On the fourth day, we all returned one last time to the Wyrdwood North High School gymnasium. Violet and her team had transformed it yet again, adding tiny dancing rainbows that shone from crystals hung at the windows near the ceiling. She'd replaced the original flower arrangements with roses—a mix of white and dark blue. Their scent gave the room a rich and sensual atmosphere.

As soon as we'd realized the treaty would be signed, Corona, Mom, and I went shopping for appropriate celebratory attire—on Jake's card, of course. Corona bought an adorable turquoise dress. Mom chose a Boho skirt and sparkle-enhanced sweater. For me, I'd wanted to buy the simple, long-sleeved sweater dress I found in midnight blue. Mom, however, insisted that I get the rose-colored cocktail dress with the beaded bodice and knee-length chiffon skirt that looked amazing on me, but that pushed the boundaries of what I would usually wear in public. She pulled rank, and so—to please her—I took it home along with a new pair of satin ballerina flats, and wore them to the signing. I received many compliments on it.

Truth was, I felt pretty.

Once again, we sat around the table, but one thing was different. We had a treaty to sign. The Thu and the Fomor had come to an accord the previous day and were both ready to put magickal pen to paper.

An attendant who kept his eyes lowered the whole time produced the finalized treaty and fancy pens for both signatories.

Lenore and Rebus stood side-by-side and signed simultaneously.

My throat clenched with emotion, and I blinked back happy tears. There would be no war.

Once they'd set aside their pens, Rebus and Lenore shook hands. The room erupted in a giant cheer, and everyone stood to give the two leaders an ovation. I clapped so hard, my hands hurt.

After several minutes of celebration, Rebus quieted the room by raising his hand.

A series of shushing noises traveled through the crowd, ending in silence.

Rebus and Lenore's eyes met, and they both nodded. I could have sworn they even smiled a little. Then, they turned toward me.

"Shall I?" Lenore asked Rebus. He bowed his head in acquiescence.

Lenore folded her hands in front of her solar plexus and said, "Viviane, you have brought peace to us all. You've begun the process of reparation and healing for a breach that has festered for far too long." Emotion tightened her mouth, and her eyes shone. She had to pause.

Rebus, seeing this, said, "We felt that it was only right that you too should find the ultimate happiness today."

"Oh, I'm very happy," I said, but he lifted his hand.

"Let me finish," he said, and I saw both kindness and affection—maybe even pride—in his eyes. "We think that there could be no better day for you to enter into a union of your own."

I didn't understand, but then Colin stepped up beside me and took my hand.

"All our families are here, now," Lenore said, having found her voice again. "Why not give us a second reason to celebrate?"

"You mean?"

Colin said, "Let's get married. Right now."

I wanted to agree, but... There was always a "but" wasn't there? Nothing was ever perfect. I said, "I can't. Not without Abram."

"I love you," Colin said, and he waved his hand to indicate the far side of the room.

Abram stood there, grinning like a happy hound, with Mom on his arm. He was dressed in formal wear, the human variety—a dream come true, in my eyes.

Colin whispered, "Your mother insisted."

Happiness swelled inside me, and I realized there weren't any "buts" left.

"Yes," I said, my voice capable of little more than a whisper. "Let's get married."

Colin picked me up in a hug and swung me around. Another round of cheers went up as everyone breathed again.

Back on my feet, I promised Colin I'd be right back then ran to my grandfather. We hugged for a long time.

"You okay?" he asked, his soft cheek against my ear.

"More than okay," I replied. "You?"

"Better now."

I whispered, "So you know about Mom? It's weird, right?"

He pulled back to look at my face, his old-man fingers gently brushing loose tendrils of my hair away. "Yeah, but I recognize her soul."

Grandpa never failed to surprise me when he said things like that. It was so out of character for him—and yet, it wasn't. I was overcome with love for him.

"Grandpa?" I looked into his eyes. "Will you give me away?"

His eyes crinkled and shone. "It'd be my honor,

young lady." He looked over my shoulder and added, "I believe they're waiting for you."

I paused only long enough to give Mom a hug and a kiss on the cheek.

"I'm so happy," she said.

"Me too."

Then I linked my arm with Grandpa's, and we walked back toward the other side of the gym where Colin, Lenore, Rebus, and Violet were waiting for us. As we went, I only had eyes for Colin.

Violet raised her voice to be heard, and the crowd took notice. She said, "Today is a day that will go down in history as a day of union, of love, and of family. The hand-fasting of Viviane Lenore Rose and Aubrey mac Bres will stand as a symbol of two families—two hearts— becoming one. If anyone in this room is not fully committed to supporting this union, I ask that you now leave." She paused, waiting.

Everyone held their breath. During the pause, Grandpa and I arrived. He kissed my forehead and let me go. I stepped up to stand facing Colin. Rebus stood behind him, and Lenore moved into position behind me.

When no one walked out, Violet nodded her satisfaction and asked us, "Shall we begin?"

Both Colin and I said, "Yes, please."

Violet pulled a braided cord from her pocket—one strand was red, one black, and one white. "Hold hands." She wrapped the cord around our clasped hands and tied a knot in it. As she did, she spoke in a voice fueled by magick and meant to be heard by gods.

"Two souls. Two hearts. Two minds. Two families. You've come together to create a union that will bring you healing, prosperity, and happiness. We ask that you tell us your dreams for the future."

A glow radiated out from us, warm and comforting.

Violet asked, "Aubrey, would you like to start?"

He nodded without taking his eyes off me. "Viviane," he said. "Viv. I knew you were the one for me the moment we first met, even though I didn't know who *I* was at the time. You brought me back to life, and I'm so grateful because now I get to spend it with you. My dream for us includes a home, children, and many long years of rowdy family meals and quiet, intimate moments. I can't even imagine my life without you in it. My commitment to you is a commitment to my own happiness." His face tightened with emotion. "No matter what happens, you will always be mine. Never forget that."

I whispered, "Never."

Violet waited a moment to be sure he was done, then she turned to me. "Viviane, tell us *your* dreams for your future."

I gathered my thoughts and my emotions so I could speak then said, "I never dared to dream that any of this could be happening. Not really. I could only see a gray future for us, even though we'd be together—or so I hoped. Malum was casting this dark shadow on us, and now—

finally—I feel like it's lifted. Do I dare dream?" A smile spread on my face. "I do. In my dreams, we are never alone. We know—beyond a shadow of a doubt—that we are loved. And we never have to hide who we are—not from each other." I squeezed his hands. "In my dreams, no one can ever separate us again." My nose tickled with tears.

Colin whispered, "Never."

I could sense the attention of everyone in the room on me, their compassion and sympathy. Their love.

Again, Violet waited to make sure I was done, then she squared herself to us. She put both her hands on top of ours—directly on the braid that she'd tied there. "This braid," she said, "binds you together so that you might share sunny days and clement nights. So that you might shelter in one another during storms and darkness. The red strand is the life blood that flows through you both, from your ancestors, and into your descendants. The black strand is the trouble you will overcome together, because life is not without challenge and sorrow. The white strand shines its light upon you so that you can always see one another even when nothing else is clear."

Violet took a deep breath, then looked out to the crowd. "What true love has created, let no one dismantle. Residents of Wyrdwood, Gehenna, Apfallon, and beyond, take note. Viviane and Aubrey's union weaves families, minds, hearts, and souls together into a whole that will be stronger, healthier, and longer lasting than its threads."

Violet paused, then shouted at the top of her lungs, "Meallaibh ur naidheachd!" I was startled and had no idea what that meant—until the crowd echoed her. Some shouted the same phrase, others simply shouted, "Congratulations!" I burst out laughing.

And just like that, Colin and I were married. I turned to him and asked, "Are you ready for an adventure?"

He grinned and replied, "I am so ready."

The room around us began to shift and change. Long dining tables appeared, carried in by attendants wearing the colors of Apfallon. Food and drink came next, and the celebration was underway. The Fomor provided the musical entertainment, which proved to be much more sophisticated and fun than what I'd seen in Gehenna.

We danced all evening, and I'd never had my back patted so many times as each person there took a moment to congratulate us.

When it came time to leave, Colin informed me that my great-grandmother was offering us a suite in Gliton Manor where we could honeymoon. Everyone showered us with cherry blossom petals as we left the gym. A white limo waited for us there, ready to take us to Fortunate Lake and the boat to Apfallon.

Once the limo doors were closed, Colin and I had our first moment of quiet. I nestled in the circle of his arm, thinking about our past, our present, and our future. He too was silent, lost in thought, his cheek pressed to my head.

I asked, "Did you remember to pack your tooth-brush?"

I felt his laughter shake his body. He replied, "Yes, ma'am. No halitosis monkey here." He dipped his head and kissed me with all his beautiful heart.

❀❀❀

The End for Now

Appendix

Moira Gliton—a.k.a. Bella Rosenblum—sat upon an ancient stone in the grove of oak trees, a ray of sunlight filtering in through the autumn-colored leaves. Occasionally, one such golden or scarlet leaf would drift down from above and join its siblings upon the forest floor.

A chill had snuck into the air, but Moira didn't notice. She was lost in memories.

Colin and Viviane had arrived at the safe house the previous evening, having escaped Nathan's assault. The day had dawned clear and bright, belying the danger that lurked just beyond the horizon.

Bella was folding Viviane's jeans, fresh out of the dryer. She placed them on the pile with the rest of her clothes. It gave Bella pleasure to perform such a simple task for the young woman, but it also poked a wound that had never quite healed and reminded her of how much she had missed. She envied the Normals who could live their lives and raise their children without ancestral complications. They formed their little families and stayed together their entire lives—if they so chose. That wasn't how it was for Bella and her family. At each generation, the connection to Apfallon had torn the family apart and sent them scattering into dark corners to hide. Bella's family had been hunted and tormented. That was what happened when you fell in love with a prince from another realm.

Ajani appeared at Bella's elbow. "I'll take those to her," he offered, indicating the freshly laundered clothes.

Bella smiled up at the tall man. She stepped back and watched him pick up the pile. Her gratitude toward him swelled in her chest. She couldn't have done any of it without him. He'd never left her side and had been loyal throughout, despite the danger. He'd saved her life and Viviane's.

As had Jax. Jaxon Bellonescu had been the first loss of many. War always produced casualties, and Jax had known his was a suicide mission. It didn't make his death any easier for Bella to bear.

"Ajani," she said quietly before he could leave the room.

He looked back, curiosity on his quirky face.

Bella found herself at a sudden loss for words. The only one that popped to the surface was, "Thanks," but it came with a thousand unspoken others.

Ajani bowed his head. "As always, it is my pleasure." The affection in his gaze was unmistakable.

Bella returned to the kitchen to find Colin there with his head in the refrigerator. "Don't forage," she scolded. "I'm making a nice breakfast." She stopped at the stove to flip the bacon frying in the cast iron skillet.

"Yes, ma'am," he replied, sounding chipper. He closed the refrigerator and took a seat at the bar.

"Where's Viviane?" Bella asked.

"In the shower."

"Good." Bella said. "I need to talk to you. I'm furious with you."

"Why?" Colin asked.

Bella didn't look at him. The bacon

popped and crackled. She set the tongs aside and put a second pan on to heat. Voice low and firm, she said, "Do you realize how close you came to getting her killed?" She cast him a glance but couldn't bear to look at him longer than that. She wanted to explode his head.

"Nathanatos wouldn't have done that."

"Don't be a fool, Aubrey," said Bella, through clenched teeth. "Your brother is unpredictable, at best." She turned on him then, and her eyes flashed with fury. She channeled her anger into a hiss, managing somehow to keep her voice down. "What made you think he wouldn't kill her in front of you, just to remove any desire you have to stay away?"

Colin hesitated, then said, "He knew if he did anything to her, he'd have to kill me too."

"And you, you arrogant idiot, assumed that he wants you alive?" Bella slapped her fragile hand down on the edge of the sink. She turned away, rubbing her thumb over her stinging palm. She had

eggs to mix and cheese to grate.

"I didn't know he'd snatch her," Colin retorted.

"Pfah!" Bella dismissed him with a gesture. "You left her clues so she wouldn't give up trying to find you, and Nathan figured it out."

"It all turned out okay," Colin said. "She's here with us, safe and sound. Nathan's lost this battle. We can disappear and live happily ever after. Viviane is my betrothed. I had to have her with me."

The flush that had risen to Bella's cheeks with her anger drained away at the sound of his words. She made an effort to keep her voice even as she said, "You realize... You know...she can't go with us. Right?" She broke an egg on the edge of a bowl. It collapsed in her hand, spilling yoke and white upon her fingers.

"Of course, she can," said Colin. "She has to go with us. She belongs to me."

Bella dropped the eggshell into the sink and reached for a towel. She faced Colin and reasoned, "That is exactly why she can't go with us. With her parentage, we can't risk your father ever getting his hands on her."

She lowered her voice, "He'd use her to break the curse and start a war."

"She'll be safer with me, and that's that," said Colin.

Bella felt a panic coming on. This was the moment she'd feared the most when she had first learned of Colin and Viviane's relationship. He was going to drag her down with him.

Bella leaned close to Colin and lowered her voice to a whisper. "Please. I'm begging you. Don't get her caught in the crossfire. She doesn't deserve it. She's innocent. You chose to be here. You determined your own fate with your eyes wide open to the repercussions. She doesn't have that luxury. You're dragging her into something she's isn't equipped to understand or survive."

Colin laughed as if at a child with an overactive imagination. "Your bacon's burning, Bella."

"Good morning," Viviane said from the doorway. "Something smells deli-

cious."

Bella backed away from Colin and put a smile on her face. "Good morning, dear. Come in. I'm making breakfast. Coffee?" She watched as Viviane and Colin exchanged smiles, then a kiss. He pulled her into the circle of his arms.

"Yes, that would be awesome," Viviane said. "I can get it."

Bella waved dismissively. "No, you sit down. Do you take cream or sugar?"

"Neither," answered Viviane. "Black. Can I do anything to help?"

Bella crossed to the coffee maker, and her hand shook as she upturned a clean mug. "I've got it all under control."

A shiver snaked across Bella's shoulders, bringing her back to the present. In hindsight, everything had worked out—more or less. Life was like that. It felt terrifying when you were in the thick of it, but nothing was ever quite as bad as fear predicted. Either you survived, or you didn't. And even death wasn't the end.

Bella's attention was drawn back to the water she'd poured into a concave indent on the top of the altar stone. She looked at her watch—nearly five o'clock in Wyrdwood—took a deep breath and focused her magic.

The surface of the water glowed like an opal. Bella watched events unfolding that made her heart ache. She wished she could be there in person, with her family, but that ship had embarked more than a quarter of a century prior. She would not do that to Abram Rose, the man she'd loved and who had loved her faithfully throughout his life. To him, she was dead and always would be.

"Viviane Rose"

"Colin!" Viviane called from the kitchen where she was loading a dishwasher. The room suited her with its red checkered curtains and practical butcher-block table. It looked lived in, but clean.

"What's up?" Colin asked, coming in to drop a kiss on the back of her neck.

"Can you take that tray into the living room? I think people are getting hungry."

"Sure." Colin wrapped an arm around Viviane's waist. "Leave that for now. Come sit with us. It's almost five. Nobody cares about a few dirty dishes."

"I know. I know," Viviane said. "I'm just... It's nervous energy."

Colin took her by the hand, grabbing the tray with

the other, and led her out into the living room. The decor reminded Bella of Abram's old place, but that might have been the photos on the mantelpiece and the old quilt draped over the back of the couch. It was cozy, and Bella decided to visit them there soon with a housewarming gift.

"There you are," said Gisèle.

Bella had finally begun to see her daughter instead of a stranger when she looked at the new face and body. Gisèle's signature gestures, the way she moved, the tilt of her head—all that helped. Plus, she'd cut her hair into an adorable pixie cut and had dyed it blond. She was reclaiming her identity.

"Just finishing up the dishes," Viviane said, sitting down on the couch beside Abram.

As always, Bella watched Abram for a moment, closely, looking for any sign of illness. She worried about him and the toll taken by everything that had happened. She was glad to see that he looked better, more well-rested since moving to Wyrdwood to be near Viviane. The thought of him alone in Peoria with only his golf buddies to keep him company had troubled Bella.

"What time is it?" Corona asked. She was pacing back and forth between the window and the door. A hairy pixie sat upon her shoulder—a strange little man with a tiny sarong covering him from the waist down. He was whittling a tiny piece of wood.

Abram grumbled, "She'll get here when she gets here.

Sit down, please. You're making me dizzy."

Corona harumphed and perched on the edge of a chair, turning to look at the window.

The doorbell rang.

Corona leapt up and ran to answer it. She pulled the door wide with enthusiasm, then promptly deflated. "Oh. It's you."

Bella's mother, Lenore Gliton, stood on the threshold. "Good to see you too, young lady," said the elderly woman. "Help me in." She leaned heavily on a cane when in Reality. The weight of Normality weighed on her there. Sometimes, instead of expending magick to support herself, she let her age show through. Whether it was self-punishment or a commitment to realism, Bella didn't know.

Viviane rose to greet her. "Welcome, Lenore. I'm so glad you could make it. Is Kushala with you?"

"She's getting our present out of the car. Girl, you should go carry it for her. She's rickety." Lenore pointed a finger at Corona.

For the next few minutes, the scene could have been any family home at Thanksgiving or Christmas. Conversations overlapped, drinks were poured, and snacks were consumed. Someone turned the television on, got yelled at, and turned it off again. A pile of presents in the corner grew by one, and Lenore's wife joined the party.

Colin said, "If anyone was magickal, it was David Bowie."

"C'mon. Everybody knows he was kith," said Kushala. "Me, I'd nominate Björk."

"Tori Amos," said Gisèle. "No doubt."

"Tell me somethin' I didn't know," said Corona.

Viviane commented, "Can you imagine what it must be like to be magickal and famous? It'd be so hard!"

"Joanna Newsom," Corona offered.

"Who?" asked everyone else.

Corona said, "Joanna… Never mind. Hold on, I've got one of her songs on my phone. You'll see."

"I think I know who she is," said Viviane. "Plays the harp, right?"

Abram asked, "Who's the fella who sings 'You're Beautiful'?"

"The Monkees," suggested Lenore.

Abram shook his head. "No, not them. That pasty-faced British fella."

Kushala scowled, "Much as I loved them, The Monkees were all marketing, no magick. What about Laurie Anderson. Oh, Supermaaaaaan…"

"Stevie Nicks," said Lenore, "once visited Wyrdwood, I think. I swear I saw her in the diner down on Ocean View. She got apple pie."

"You're beautiful!" Abram bellowed. "You're beautiful! You're beautiful! Ad nauseum. I nominate *that* guy for *least* magickal."

The doorbell rang.

Everyone stopped talking.

"I'll get it," Colin said. He was up before anyone else could move—even Corona.

The door opened, letting a new stream of sunlight into the room. A figure entered.

Amalia, the Midwife, stood there with a wriggling Ivy in her arms. She scanned the faces in the room with cool detachment until she spotted Viviane.

Viviane started to rise, but Amalia said, "Don't get up. I'm not staying." The Midwife crossed the room without acknowledging anyone else and handed the baby to Viviane.

"Hi, sweetheart," said Viviane to Ivy. "I'm so glad to see you." The love shining in Viviane's eyes was bright enough to light all of Wyrdwood.

Amalia pressed her palm to Viviane's forehead, as if to bless her, and said, "Congratulations. You're now a mother." She briefly rested her hand on Viviane's shoulder, then turned around and left the way she'd come.

"No standing on ceremony with that one," commented Kushala with a shake of her head.

The family gathered around Viviane, Colin right at her side. So many loving hands touched baby fingers, baby toes, baby head.

When the baby became fussy, Viviane nurse little Ivy with her family around her. Colin wrapped his arms around his wife and child.

"She's ours now," he said.

Viviane replied, "And we're hers."

"Amalia"

The women summoned Amalia, but they had waited too long. By the time Amalia entered the bedroom, she knew the baby was gone. She stood in the doorway, surveying the red-faced, wide-eyed women gathered around the straining mother.

Such was birth. Such was death. A drama witnessed by simple folk who understood none of it.

Amalia could smell the fear, blood, and amniotic fluid—thick, steamy, sweaty. She held her face impassive and crossed to the bed.

The women spread the mother's legs and pushed back her gown, exposing her to Amalia's eyes. The child's head was crowning, its hair black and slick.

Efficient, Amalia set down her bag of tools, then took the mother's ankles and pulled her to the edge of the bed. With only her hands, she directed the women to hold the mother's feet in a stirrup position; then she knelt and went to work.

The mother's flesh had already begun to tear, so it was no great challenge to cut a wider opening, push in her thin strong fingers, and pull the babe from its tomb.

It slid out with a surge of blood and lay on the bed between its mother's legs, soundless, lifeless.

Gasps came from all corners of the room, and the mother called for answers with growing anguish. Expression unchanging, Amalia met and held the mother's eyes until she saw understanding dawn in them. The mother dropped her head back to release a scream of sorrow.

Amalia wrapped the infant in the blanket provided her. She whispered in its ear, a blessing that would give it easier passage next time. Through pursed lips, she blew her breath across the child's face, freeing its soul to go, to relinquish that impossible life, and to return to the source from which it came. She felt the departure of the child's essence and knew its destiny—though great—awaited elsewhere.

Standing, she handed the swaddled corpse to a gray-haired woman to her left. The woman took it to the arms of its mother.

Around the room, the women wailed.

While the mother was distracted, clutching her child to her breast, Amalia saw to the delivery of the placenta. That accomplished, she dug in her bag for a needle and thread. She stitched with calm precision. Each dip and tug of the needle, each pull of the thread, wove a new fate for the mother. Another chance, with another baby. The next one would, perhaps, stay. Amalia did not know everything.

When Amalia rose, she left her mess behind. Cleaning up was someone else's duty. She stowed her tools in her bag, then went to the doorway.

The elder woman was waiting there for her with a stack of bills. The woman said nothing, her voice stolen by her grief.

Amalia took the bills. "Next time, call me sooner." She walked out.

"Chance"

Chance stood seething on the threshold to Gehenna. If he continued, he'd begin his time of reflection prior to the transmigration of his soul into a new life. If he went back—and that was an option—he would be trapped in a half-existence between realms, a ghost without any substance or power to influence events in Reality. He'd be nothing.

They'd destroyed his body with fire. He had no corpus to go back to. The snap of his silver cord when it had come free still vibrated within him.

To reincarnate or to slowly fade away as a ghost—it wasn't much of a choice. The pain echoed in his head where Viviane had bludgeoned him. The pain in his ego was worse. He never would have guessed she had it in her to kill him. He'd thought she loved him.

"Bitch," he said aloud. The whispering wraiths behind him stirred. Their scratching egged him on, and he threw back his head and shouted with fury, "Fucking bitch!" He growled and tensed every muscle in his body. It helped, and afterward, he was able to relax.

Gehenna had been his home his entire life, but it wasn't a homecoming. He'd lost everything. His wife. His daughter. His future.

A dark spot on the ground caught his eye, and he bent to pick it up. A black button. Solid and normal, it seemed the perfect symbol for his situation. It was lost, but it still had an inherent purpose.

Chance stuck it in his pants pocket and lifted his chin. He said, "There's always next Samhain." And on that note, he entered Gehenna.

Thanks for Reading

WW07032020

If you enjoyed this story, *please* take a moment to give it a review. It's the kindest thing you can do for the authors you love and who love you back.

Free gifts. The Wyrdwood Historical Society presents two free stories.

"Nurse Magdaleine" — free short story ebook

"Charlie Darwin" — free novella ebook

Download them at

http://wyrdwoodangel.com/freebies/

Join our growing community by signing up for the Wyrdwood email list. We'll send instructions for how to connect with other magickal readers just like you.

Sign up now for the Wyrdwood mailing list.

Know anyone you think would like this story?

Please let them know about it! They'll appreciate that you did and so will I.

And now, here's a sneak preview of the next novel release from Wyrdwood.

Wyrdwood Grave Dirt Series, Book #1

Sneak Preview

The second trilogy out of Wyrdwood follows mortician Isabella Fandelli's efforts to solve her mother's murder.

Like most daughters, Isabella Fandelli had a chafing relationship with her mother. Those apron strings simply would not break, no matter how hard Isabella struggled against them. Leaving for college in the big city—Portland—and putting distance between them had helped a little. Cleona Jenice Fandelli, Isabella's mother, had a plan for her daughter that involved her taking over the family business. Cleona wanted to retire to Arizona, nest in a little clay-roofed adobe bungalow and write romance novels in the final chapter of her life. And that meant *someone* had to take over the Fandelli business.

The trouble was twofold: 1) Isabella had big career plans of her own, and 2) *whenever* Isabella returned home for a visit she reverted to the angry, rebellious teenager she'd been before leaving.

Isabella told her mother, "You won. You got me here. Kind of extreme tactic, though, don't you think? The moment I graduate, you guilt me back home." She was irritated, my young Isabella, pacing back and forth, shoving her hands into her hair until it was standing up like a halo of black lace. She said, "I never should have taken that money. I'd be two years ahead of the curve if I'd just paid for school on my own. Hell, who knew I could even do that? I didn't. Not until it was too late. Mom! I wasted two years of my life pursuing *your* dream because I didn't know I could pursue my own. You never told me that, Mom. You never told me I could do whatever I wanted. Not once. I had to learn that on my own, and I'm pretty god-damned pissed about that too. Just sayin'."

Her mother, a Fandelli by marriage not birth, did not reply. An Italian mother would have risen from the grave to have the last word.

Isabella deflated with a big sigh. She was gentle as she brushed aside a roaming lock of hair on her mother's corpse. Dark and luscious, Cleona's hair had once curled with abandon. Quite recently, however, it had lost its soul. Literally. Isabella had inherited that hair, like her curvy figure, from her mother and the DNA of African ancestors.

Isabella could not look away from her mother's slack face as she pulled the stainless-steel cart closer and dipped her fingers in the water contained in the steel washing bowl. It had grown cold. Isabella picked up the bowl and carried it to the utility sink, dumped it, and re-filled it. She added lavender-scented soap—her mother's favorite.

When she returned to her mother's side, she left the dark thoughts and feelings behind, soaked a wash cloth in the soapy water, and began to clean her mother's body one inch at a time as she had seen her mother do for others.

If she'd been preparing a stranger, Isabella would have worn latex gloves, but not with her own mother. She did not need that barrier between her and her mother's beloved skin.

"You sure you don't want to get a contractor in to do that?" Isabella's sister Bluciel leaned against the door frame, on the threshold to the embalming room. That child was always stylish, and even in deep mourning, she had chosen to wear a rich shade of burgundy. With her hair dark and thick like their father's—he'd been a Fandelli through and through—Bluciel was far more put-together than Isabella.

Isabella did not look up from her work when she replied, "I'm fine." The thought of turning her mother over to a stranger must have made Isabella ill, and Cleona would have been mortified. The washing had meaning. It was one final task Isabella could do for her mother.

Bluciel kept her eyes averted and her arms crossed tightly over her chest. She was not as stoic as Isabella. A poetic soul, she said, "My heart aches in ways I didn't know it could."

Isabella's face tightened briefly, and she sniffed.

They stayed like that until Isabella was nearly done. Bluciel remained out of respect and caring for their mother, a silent observer. Isabella finished the ritual, washing all the way down to her mother's toes—one inch at a time.

Isabella asked, "Do you want me to get someone else in to do the make-up?"

Bluciel shook her head with tiny movements. Her lips didn't know what expression to form. "I can't."

"You don't have to."

"I don't know how you..."

Isabella touched the back of her hand to her mother's cheek. "It's what she'd have wanted." The words came out so quietly, they were almost inaudible.

Bluciel shifted her weight and pushed away from the door frame. "Did you talk to Mrs. Horvat?"

Morana Horvat was a force of nature. She could dig a grave faster than anyone. She was a stout woman of

Slavic origin, stoic, reliable, and certified in all the funeral equipment. Mrs. Horvat claimed that tending graves ran in her family and that her father had been a grave guardian in Cerbia. The Fandelli family relied heavily on her to manage the mechanics of burials and to keep the graveyard maintained.

Isabella picked up the water bowl and took it to the sink. "I assumed we'd cremate."

Tension sharpened Bluciel's voice. She said, "No, Iz. She didn't want that. She wanted to be buried in the cemetery."

"We can still do that. The ashes—"

"No, Iz. She. Didn't. Want. That." Bluciel's agitation made every word an attack. "You can't just come home after all this time and..."

"And what?"

"And do things however you want. Mom was afraid of the retort." It was true. As she'd gotten older, more introspective, Cleona had come to hate the burning. It wasn't so much fear as it was an existential disagreement with the destruction of molecules and DNA. Cleona wanted her body returned to the earth in its most natural form.

Isabella turned to face her sister. "Don't be ridiculous. Mom? It was her job to—"

"Not for years. She hired a guy to come in and handle the furnace. Mom wouldn't go anywhere near it."

That made Isabella pause. She had been away for six years at college, a quarter of her life. And in that time, the world of Fandelli Mortuary had continued on without her. Her connection to her family had fallen by the wayside.

Cleona had suspected that her daughter had wanted it that way.

"You should pick out a bed for her then," Isabella said with casual disinterest, but she watched as Bluciel turned and walked away. The look on her face told a different story.

Alone with her mother's body, Isabella mocked her sister. "Sure, Iz. I can do that. No problem." She rinsed out the wash cloth in the sink and tossed it into the laundry bag, then unzipped and stepped out of her coveralls, adding them to the bleach pile as well.

"Isabella?" The voice—a voice that Isabella recognized—caused her to halt where she was, frozen. In fact, she'd been hoping to hear it and dreading it. "Isabella? Are you there? Can you hear me, honey?"

"I'm here, Mom," Isabella's mouth twisted with grief. "I hear you."

TO BE CONTINUED...

About the Author

Angel Leigh McCoy worn many faces, told many stories, loved many people, and lived many lives. Through it all, writing has been her one constant.

Angel is a spark of creative force behind the darkly fanciful Wyrdwood project and the epic Dire Multiverse.

She's an award-winning video game writer, having worked on "CONTROL," IGN's Game of the Year 2019. Prior to that, she spent ten years weaving intricate tales for millions of *Guild Wars 2* fans. As a writer for White Wolf's *World of Darkness*, she created stories about vampires, changelings, mages, and werewolves.

Receive an alert when Angel's next Wyrdwood book is available.

WyrdwoodAngel.com

⨦⨦⨦

Copyright

Hexing the Moon

Print ISBN-13: 978-1-950427-10-9